The MYSTERY of the
MISSING EVERYTHING

The MYSTERY of the MISSING EVERYTHING

BEN H. WINTERS

HARPER

An Imprint of HarperCollinsPublishers

Library of Congress Cataloging-in-Publication Data
Winters, Ben H.
    The mystery of the missing everything / Ben H. Winters.—1st ed.
        p.   cm.
    Summary: When a treasured trophy disappears from the display case at Mary Todd
Lincoln Middle School and the principal cancels the eagerly anticipated eighth grade class
trip, Bethesda Fielding has no choice but to solve the mystery.
    ISBN 978-0-06-196544-9 (tr. bdg.)
    [1. Mystery and detective stories. 2. Middle schools—Fiction. 3. Schools—
Fiction.] I. Title.
PZ7.W7667My 2011   2011010167
[Fic]—dc22   CIP
                                                                          AC

Typography by Alison Klapthor
11   12   13   14   15   CG/RRDB   10 9 8 7 6 5 4 3 2 1
❖
First Edition

For
Raedina Winters

Table of Contents

1

The Case of the Missing Trophy

The funny thing about clues is, if you don't know you're solving a mystery, then they're not clues. They're just . . . stuff.

So when the random piece of plastic poked Bethesda Fielding in the foot as she walked into school on that clear and cloudless Tuesday morning in September, she didn't gasp and shout "Aha!" Neither did she stroke her chin and say "very interesting—very interesting indeed." Bethesda wasn't in detective mode. She didn't know there was a mystery to be solved. Not yet.

It was, by all appearances, an entirely ordinary day. Bethesda woke to her Three Ducks Quacking alarm clock; she got dressed and plucked her glasses from the bedside table; she wrangled her reddish-tannish hair into twin butterfly barrettes; she tumbled downstairs to the kitchen for breakfast . . . everything exactly the same as always.

Bethesda biked to school along the regular route: Left down Chesterton, soft right on Dunwiddie, a long easy downhill glide, feet off the pedals, until the final right onto Friedman Street. Bethesda listened to her iPod while she biked, bopping her head to this cool D.C. pop band, Title Tracks, that her friend Tenny Boyer had gotten her into over the summer. After chaining up her bike, Bethesda paused by the big gnarled oak tree that stood guard by the front doors of Mary Todd Lincoln Middle School, and gave it a friendly pat for luck.

A little blue-and-green swallow sat chirping happily in the crook of the tree. Bethesda had seen this cheerful character around a lot the first couple weeks of school, but not at all in the last few days. She smiled to see the sweet bird again. The sun sparkled in the golden leaves; the autumn breeze teased into the sleeves of Bethesda's lime-green fall jacket.

And then, as Bethesda pulled open the big main door and stepped inside, something jabbed the thin sole of her black-and-white Chuck Taylor sneakers.

"Ouch," she said softly, though it didn't really hurt.

She paused there, just inside the threshold of the school, to crouch and pick the thing up. It was some cast-off piece of junk, that's all, a small hunk of off-white plastic, chipped and dirty, about the size of an apple slice.

But Bethesda wasn't in detective mode—not yet. She didn't snatch the dingy little crescent and hold it up to the light for further examination. She didn't preserve it carefully in a sandwich bag and pronounce it to be a most intriguing clue, indeed. She didn't really have time to do much of anything, because the next second, Shelly Schwartz came hurtling from the other end of the hallway, waving her hands.

"Oh my *god*! Bethesda!" Shelly yelped, grinning and seizing her by the arm. "Do you *know* what's going on?"

Bethesda grinned back at Shelly. Eighth graders, in general, *love* it when something is going on. She jammed the hunk of plastic into the front pocket of her backpack and allowed herself to be dragged down the hall. In that instant, the dingy, yellowed piece of hallway flotsam was transformed from a random piece of junk into a vital clue. Whether Bethesda Fielding would figure that out in time—and whether she could solve the bizarre and baffling mystery that was about to consume her life—remained to be seen.

✦ ✦ ✦

No one at Mary Todd Lincoln had ever seen Principal Van Vreeland quite this angry.

Oh, she'd been angry before. Many times. She had been *very* angry last year, when Ms. Finkleman's seventh-grade Music Fundamentals class had tied for second in the All-County Choral Corral, instead of pulverizing Grover Cleveland to a fine dust with their rock and roll magnificence, as she had specifically commanded them to do. She had been *extremely* angry two years ago on International Day, when the sauerkraut specially prepared by the lunch lady, Mrs. Doonan, had sent the deputy superintendent of schools to the hospital for a week. She had been *exceptionally* angry three semesters ago, when Mr. Kleban, the sixth-grade math teacher, had turned out to be an unemployed actor who printed his teaching certificate off the internet.

But now, as she glowered down from the stage of the auditorium, gripping the top of the lectern like she was ready to tear it off, it was clear that the principal had achieved an unprecedented level of angriness.

"Whoever committed this crime will *pay*," Principal Van Vreeland pronounced, sweeping her furious gaze across the audience. "You. Will. *Pay*." Assistant Principal

Jasper Ferrars, seated to her left, twitched visibly and mopped his high forehead with a cloth handkerchief.

"Yikes," Bethesda whispered to Shelly.

"Seriously."

The girls were seated in the back of the auditorium with the other eighth graders. Bethesda actually would have preferred to sit closer to the front, because she was kind of short and didn't like to miss anything. But as the oldest kids in school, eighth graders had a natural and inalienable right to sit way, way in the back during all-school assemblies. And if there was one thing Bethesda liked about being an eighth grader, it was finally doing all the things only eighth graders get to do.

"And as for the *rest* of you!" the principal thundered, thumping the top of the lectern with the flat of her hand. "If you know anything about this, do *not* keep it to yourself. I assure you, you do not want to share in the punishment when the criminal is found."

The auditorium was totally, eerily quiet. Yes, their principal got angry with dismaying frequency, but words like "crime" and "criminal" were something new. No one giggled; no one snapped gum; no one made loud gross noises and then looked around innocently to see who had made the loud gross noises. Mr. Darlington, Bethesda's science teacher, shifted anxiously in his seat, folding and unfolding his long legs. Kindly Mrs. Howell shook her head sadly, evincing a grandmotherly disappointment in whoever had gotten up to such shenanigans. Even gruff Mr. Melville—who usually reacted to the principal's melodramatic pronouncements with an audible, dismissive snort—sat gravely, his arms folded across the vast expanse of his stomach.

"*Somebody* stole that trophy," the principal continued. "That person will be found, and that beautiful trophy will be returned to its rightful owner! Me!" Mr. Ferrars coughed meaningfully. "Oh. I mean Ms. Preston, of course."

Bethesda looked over at Pamela Preston, seated one row up and three seats over, unscrewing the cap from a bottle of pomegranate seltzer. You weren't allowed to eat or drink during school assemblies, but apparently Pamela had special permission because of the circumstances. Pamela was as pretty and put-together as always, but this morning her perfect light-blue eyes were puffy from crying. She sat stiff and upright, taking slow, measured sips of her seltzer, and even her blond curls seemed more tightly coiled than usual. It was as if her whole body was working overtime to keep her from breaking down into sobs.

Over the weekend Pamela had won the first-place all-around trophy at the first county gymnastics meet of the year, and yesterday the trophy had been ceremoniously installed in a glass case in the Achievement Alcove, a little nook at the end of the Front Hall, by the doors of the Main Office. And then, sometime after school, someone had smashed the glass case and stolen it. This was a pretty horrible thing to do, all the more so because Pamela's trophy was the first and only trophy ever won at Mary Todd Lincoln Middle School, not counting the Let's Go Mental for Dental Hygiene trophy—but that was awarded by Molar Brothers Toothpaste, and every school in the county got one.

"One person has the key, and one person grants access to this building after four o'clock, and that's this person right here," continued Principal Van Vreeland, pointing a long, trembling finger at the assistant principal, who gulped and looked down at his feet, like he was the one in trouble. "Whoever committed this heinous act is guilty not only of theft, but of trespassing, breaking and entering, and probably a bunch of other stuff I haven't even thought of yet!"

Listening to this seething monologue, glancing again at Pamela, Bethesda Fielding felt an eager excitement building in her gut.

A terrible crime!

An innocent victim!

A *mystery*!

Some people were famous for their athletic prowess (like Guy Ficker and Bessie Stringer), some people were known to be amazing at art (like Marisol Pierce and Lisa Deckter), and some people were known for inexplicably falling down a lot (like Braxton Lashey, or . . . well, basically that was just Braxton). Bethesda got really good grades, and did a ton of clubs and stuff, but there had never been a Famous Fact about her, not really—until last semester, when she'd dug up the shocking rock and roll past of their boring Band and Chorus teacher, Ms. Finkleman.

Of course, what she discovered turned out to be completely wrong, and the whole incident turned into a monstrous disastrotastrophe.

But the whole experience had left Bethesda obsessed with mystery solving. That summer, at Camp Fairweather, she'd huddled under the covers with a flashlight, absorbing Nancy Drew and Agatha Christie; back home, she'd stayed up late with her parents, eating popcorn and watching Charlie Chan and Sherlock

Holmes in black and white. Bethesda didn't like to be arrogant, but she knew that if anyone could crack the Case of the Missing Trophy, it was her. Bethesda's big toe, snug in the rubber tip of her Chuck Taylor sneaker, bopped rapidly against the battered metal leg of her auditorium seat.

Wrap it up, Van Vreeland, she thought. *I've got to start digging for clues.*

But the principal wasn't done, and she'd saved the worst for last. "Until such time as the perpetrator comes forward," she hissed. "I am revoking school funding for all class trips and extracurricular activities."

Bethesda's toe stopped bopping. She stared at Shelly, who stared back, gape-mouthed with distress. *All* class trips and extracurriculars?

"No way!" shouted Guy Ficker.

"You can't do that," Hayley Eisenstein pleaded.

But it was Rory Daas who stood up and hollered what Bethesda was thinking—what they were all thinking: "What about Taproot Valley?"

Of all the eighth graders, only a quiet girl named Reenie Maslow didn't seem concerned. She stayed scrunched down low in her seat, as she had been for the entire assembly, a book open and balanced in her lap.

Of course Reenie didn't get it. She was new this year. She didn't understand about Taproot Valley. The eighth-grade class trip, scheduled for the third week in October, was five days of "outdoor education." Five days of ecology hikes, of organic gardening, of watershed science—and those were just the educational parts! It was also a week of team-building exercises, rock climbing, ropes courses, and sleeping in bunks. . . .

"No . . . no . . . ," Tucker Wilson said, dumbfounded, shaking his head from side to side. Carmine Lopez raised his hands imploringly toward the stage, like a tennis player protesting a bad call, while Bessie Stringer groaned, "Come on," and buried her face in her hands. Principal Van Vreeland just stood there, grinning wickedly, reveling in the distress she'd created.

"You *can't* cancel Taproot Valley!" protested Chester Hu, seeming genuinely confused, as if the principal had announced she was canceling gravity.

"Of course I can," she responded. "As a matter of fact, I just did."

Well, that settles it, Bethesda thought as the principal pivoted on one thin high heel and strode off the stage, Jasper rushing along behind her. *I am so solving this mystery.*

2

On the Case

On the way from the assembly to first period, Bethesda slipped away from the little knot of miserable, grumbling eighth graders to sneak a quick peek at the crime scene. But when she got to the end of the Front Hall, all she found was the massive, blue-denim-clad bulk of Janitor Steve, blocking the entrance to the Achievement Alcove like a human wall.

"Get to class, kiddo," he said, jerking his thumb. "Nothing to see here."

Craning her neck to look around the massive custodian, Bethesda caught an intriguing glimpse of the Achievement Alcove, preserved as if a murder had occurred—except that, lacking yellow police tape, Principal Van Vreeland had cordoned it off with duct tape and old typewriter ribbon.

"Hmm," Bethesda murmured softly to herself, proceeding down Hallway A toward first period. She'd find a way to get into that alcove—she knew she would. In the meantime, it was a matter of keeping her eyes and ears open, on the lookout for anything suspicious. Bethesda Fielding, Master Detective, was on the case.

Ms. Fischler didn't seem too suspicious during first period. The thin, sharp-tongued teacher in the black V-neck sweater was doing what she always did, attempting to teach advanced mathematical concepts to children with very little interest in them. As Ms. Fischler explained her patented six-stage approach to coordinate geography, her students were busy bemoaning all that Principal Van Vreeland had just stolen from them.

"Apple cider," groaned Rory, in a loud, pained whisper, his black curly hair falling over his eyes. (Over the summer a girl at tennis camp had told him he had cool hair, and Rory hadn't cut it since.) "We were going to make apple cider!"

"We were going to see snakes," groaned Bessie. "Snakes and lizards. And deer. And raccoons . . ."

"*S'mores!*" sighed Hayley, popping out her retainer so she could give full weight to the one long, woeful syllable.

"People!" snapped Ms. Fischler, drawing a slope-intercept equation on the board. "Less whining, more equation graphing."

The students picked up their pencils and set to work, but the urge to whine was not so easily contained. "You guys don't even know," said Pamela Preston after a few seconds, her voice hushed, self-pitying, and melodramatic. "You don't even know how it feels."

"Your trophy'll turn up," said Natasha Belinsky reassuringly. "Probably it's just, like, lost."

Natasha patted Pamela on the shoulder with maternal care. With a sweet, open face and dirty blond hair that fell in shampoo-commercial waves around her shoulders, Natasha was one of Pamela's best friends—although Bethesda sometimes suspected Pamela hung out with her mainly to make herself feel smarter.

"Right. Lost," said Pamela, rolling her eyes. "Or maybe the trophy came to life and ran away, and now it's living in Canada."

"Yeah! Maybe!" said Natasha brightly.

"Graph, people!" snapped Ms. Fischler. "Graph!"

"Anyone? Anyone?"

Dr. Capshaw, pacing the aisles of the English room,

waved his copy of *Animal Farm* back and forth over his head like a flag.

"Allegorical structure? Hello? Earth to second period?"

Bethesda felt bad for Dr. Capshaw, whom she liked. He had a shiny bald head and a pointy beard, like Shakespeare, and when he read aloud from *Animal Farm* he got all charged up and bounced around the room like a crazy person. Today, however, she had no time for George Orwell or for Dr. Capshaw. On the back page of her English Language Arts binder, Bethesda was composing a big list of things to think about.

Who are the prime suspects?
Who had a motive to steal the trophy?
Who had an opportunity to take it?
Who doesn't have an alibi for yesterday after school?

She looked up in time to see Dr. Capshaw toss his book down on his desk. "Okay, so we're not in the mood to talk structure," he said. "Let's try theme. How does the idea of societal injustice play out in this gripping little drama?"

"Injustice?" said Todd Spolin from under the brim of his beat-up blue baseball cap. "This Taproot Valley thing is injustice!"

"That may be so," said Dr. Capshaw, snatching off Todd's (not-permitted-in-school) ball cap and tossing it on his desk. "Who can elaborate?"

"Well, it's just lame that everyone has to suffer," Bessie answered, "because one kid did something stupid!"

"Maybe it was more than one kid," added Rory.

"Totally," agreed Ezra McClellan, who always agreed with Rory.

"Or maybe it was a teacher," said Bessie. "Maybe it was you, Dr. Capshaw!"

"It wasn't." Dr. Capshaw shot a quick look at the clock. "But we digress. Let's get back to Napoleon and Snowball."

"Wait. Who are they?" asked Natasha.

"Maybe *they* stole the trophy!" shouted Rory.

Dr. Capshaw winced and tugged on his beard. "Let's start over."

"So, okay, so today, today we're . . . moving forward with weather systems!"

Mr. Darlington said "moving forward with weather systems" like he was saying "making cotton candy and riding ponies," but nobody was buying it. The longer the day went on, the more the eighth graders had time to wallow in their collective misery, and by fourth period, they had zero interest in things like weather systems.

"Okay, so if I could—everyone? If I could . . . hello?"

It was useless. Lisa Deckter, who was on the gymnastics team with Pamela, sat with her head buried in her forearms. Bessie was back to naming kinds of animals they wouldn't get to see. ("And egrets. And foxes. And . . .") In the back of the room, Rory and Ezra were arguing over the wording of their Taproot Valley petition, and whether to send it to the school superintendent, or directly to the president.

Mr. Darlington finally requested they open their Earth Sciences workbooks and brainstorm what kind of weather event to research for their upcoming diorama project. Bethesda slid her workbook out onto her desk, but kept her full attention on her fellow students. One very promising suspect, she realized, was sitting right beside her: Guy Ficker leaned forward and directed a harsh whisper at Pamela Preston as soon as Mr. Darlington turned his back.

"This never would have happened if I had had the gym last week," Guy said. Pamela twisted around and stared at him. "Oh, *please*," she said.

"Um, children?" Mr. Darlington said, raising a long forefinger and placing it over his lips.

Bethesda knew exactly why Guy was so upset. Pamela and the rest of the gymnastics team had been given exclusive after-school use of the gym last week, to practice for their meet. Which meant that Guy hadn't had anywhere to practice his archery, even though he was also preparing for a weekend competition.

"It's not my fault gymnastics is a real, official sport," Pamela whispered icily, "and that you're the only person who does arching."

"Children?" said Mr. Darlington. "We're brainstorming? Yes?"

"It's not 'arching,'" said Guy. "It's *archery*."

"Children?"

"So, what's the big deal?" Pamela said. "So you couldn't practice your stupid bow and arrow?"

"What's the big deal?" Guy was no longer even pretending to whisper. "I shot one of the judges in the leg!"

Bethesda stopped at her locker after Mr. Darlington's class to drop off her science and English books, grab her lunch, and generally get organized for the afternoon. As she bent to tie her shoelace, Bethesda's attention was distracted by sweet, shy Marisol Pierce, a few lockers down.

"It's just so unfair," Marisol said quietly to Chester, whose locker was next to hers. Marisol, who was kind of an art prodigy, had been looking forward to the beautiful sunsets and lush green landscapes of Taproot Valley, all of which she really wanted to paint.

Bethesda lingered, crouching down and fussing with the long laces of her Chuck Taylors. As she watched, Marisol shook her head and sniffled a little; Chester, in a touching if somewhat futile gesture, handed her a wadded-up piece of loose-leaf paper to blow her nose.

"Thanks," Marisol whispered tearily, and honked into the crinkly mess.

Wow, thought Bethesda, straightening up. *She's really bummed.*

Or . . . maybe she's racked with guilt over what she's done!

Bethesda whistled a snippet of ominous music and headed to lunch. Being a detective was awesome.

"You know what'll take your mind off your troubles?" Coach Vasouvian bellowed as they filed into seventh-period gym, dropping the mesh bag of volleyballs he was lugging behind him. "Running laps!"

This was met with a chorus of groans, though it

was hardly a shocking development: any time Coach Vasouvian asked a seemingly rhetorical question, you could be pretty sure that the answer would be "running laps." Once, Ms. Zmuda had popped into the gym to ask if she could borrow a stopwatch and ended up running a quarter mile before Coach Vasouvian let her go.

As she proceeded at a decent clip around the track, her sneakers squeaking on the smudgy gym floor, Bethesda thought, *It could have been anyone. It really could have been anyone.*

Meanwhile Pamela Preston, her blond curls bobbling on her head, thought, *Poor me . . . oh, poor, poor me . . .*

. . . while Natasha Belinsky, huffing along beside Pamela, thought, *Poor Pamela . . . oh, poor, poor Pamela . . .*

. . . and Guy Ficker, way out at the front of the pack, running briskly and with perfect form, thought, *Stupid gymnastics trophy . . . serves her right . . .*

But it was Lisa Deckter, whose thoughts, if she could hear them, Bethesda the detective might have found most intriguing.

This is all my fault, Lisa thought fretfully. *It's all my fault . . .*

3

Wellington Wolf

U sually Tuesdays after school meant book club with Mrs. Howell until 3:45, followed by math-team practice in Ms. Zmuda's room. Today, of course, extracurricular activities were canceled, so Bethesda biked straight home, pedaling hard despite the dull ache in her legs from Coach Vasouvian's laps.

"Hey, Dad," Bethesda shouted as she tossed her fall jacket on the sofa and opened the hall closet where she kept school supplies. She'd been thinking about it all day as she jotted random observations on spare scraps of paper and the backs of old assignment sheets: If she was going to solve this case, she needed a good notebook in which to get herself organized. She selected a weighty, three-subject orange spiral and settled at the dining-room table. Twisting the cap off a fat Sharpie, Bethesda carefully wrote across the top of the front cover in neat black letters, officially dubbing this the SEMI-OFFICIAL CRIME-SOLVING NOTEBOOK, or S.-O.C-S.NO., or Sock-Snow for short.

"Love it," Bethesda said, holding the notebook up and grinning. Now she could do some serious mystery solving.

"All right!" said Bethesda's father, suddenly appearing at her elbow in an apron, bearing a spoon laden with burbling chili. "My taste tester is here!"

"Dad, I'm kind of—"

"Don't even start," he said. "One taste is not going to kill you. Or if it does, there is something seriously wrong with my recipe."

Bethesda's father had been making batches of chili every night for the last two weeks, all in preparation for a charity dinner in mid-October being hosted by the big fancy downtown law firm where Bethesda's mother worked. Bethesda relented, slurping a small mouthful from the big wooden spoon. "It's good, Dad."

"How would you rank it, on a scale of one to ten—one being terrible, ten being the best chili anyone has ever eaten in the history of the universe?"

"It's really, really good."

Bethesda's father frowned. "Would you mind using my scale?"

"Dad! I'm kind of working on a project here."

"Oh?" he said, plopping down next to her and waggling his eyebrows. Bethesda immediately recognized her mistake—you never said the word "project" around Bethesda's father, unless you wanted a helper. "What are we working on?"

"I'm trying to solve this mystery. And—"

"A mystery!"

"Dad. Don't say it . . ."

"Sounds like a job for Wellington Wolf!"

She *knew* he was going to say it. Wellington Wolf, Jungle P.I., was the title character of this incredibly cheesy cartoon her dad had loved as a kid. Wellington was a gruff, tough-as-nails detective with a Sherlock Holmes cap, a magnifying glass, and a streak of silver in his bristly gray fur. For the last six months, whenever Bethesda mentioned her newfound obsession with mysteries and detectives, her father insisted that Wellington Wolf was the best of them all. Her dad loved the show primarily for the god-awful puns ("Stop badgering the witness!" "But, your honor, I'm a badger!"), and Bethesda occasionally, grudgingly enjoyed watching Wellington put his big, black sniffer to the ground and crack a case.

"This is serious business, Dad."

"And what is so un-serious about Wellington Wolf?"

"Are you kidding? He's a cartoon wolf! His partner is a moose named Sergeant Moose!"

Bethesda's father waved his wooden spoon animatedly, and Bethesda laid a hand over her notebook to protect it from flying chili particles. "Say what you will about Wellington Wolf, he always gets his man. Or marmoset, or elephant, as the case may be."

"Okay, Dad. I should really get to work."

But it was too late. Her dad set down the chili spoon, leaned back in the dining-room chair, and began to recount every detail of his current favorite case, from Episode 49, "A Mole in the Hole!"

Bethesda only half listened, tapping her pen impatiently on the table. Until . . .

"Wait. Say that part again?"

"What, with the big cats? They're puns, see? You're lyin', lion! You're a cheater, chee—"

"No. The part about the man on the inside."

So her dad repeated it—how Wellington had gotten

help from a most unlikely source. Someone with special knowledge of the case. Someone with access to the crime scene.

Bethesda grinned and gave her dad an entirely unexpected kiss on the nose. That was just what Bethesda needed—she needed a man on the inside. She needed Jasper Ferrars.

4

Just One of the Reasons
Principal Van Vreeland Has Always
Hated Christmas

"**O**ne magnificent trophy. Just one, and that's all."
Principal Isabel Van Vreeland stood brooding at
the window of her office, staring off past the parking
lot into busy Friedman Street. "It's my greatest dream in
life, you know."

"I know, ma'am."

Assistant Principal Jasper Ferrars stood way over
by the door, as far away from his boss as he could get
while technically remaining in the room. He could have
reminded her that, just last week, she had said that all
she ever wanted was for Mary Todd Lincoln to achieve
the highest standardized math scores in the county. He

also could have mentioned that, *two* weeks ago, she swore that her greatest dream in life was to be the first woman to solo-kayak across the Bering Strait. But he decided, given her current state of mind, to hold his tongue.

"A golden, gleaming trophy. When I was six, I asked Santa for one, but he brought me a box of plastic pencil sharpeners instead."

"Really?"

"Just one of the reasons I've always hated Christmas."

Principal Van Vreeland sighed and settled into her big black office chair to eat her lunch of pork chops and applesauce. Jasper lingered, shifting nervously from foot to foot on the plush carpet, until—abruptly and a little too loudly—he said, "Ma'am, I have to tell you something."

"Yes?" She looked up sharply, smoothing the scarlet bib tucked into her blazer. "What is it?"

"Uh . . ." Jasper flashed a sickly smile. "Never mind, ma'am. It's nothing."

It was not, in fact, nothing. Jasper had a secret to tell the principal, a secret sure to bring the full weight of her anger down upon his head. Once in the safety of the outer office, Jasper loosened his tie and gasped for air. When was he going to tell Principal

Van Vreeland the truth? When . . . and how? Maybe he could just write her a note. And then move to Borneo and live in the jungle, with the parrots. Jasper had always loved parrots.

"Excuse me? Mr. Assistant Principal?"

Standing politely beside Mrs. Gingertee's desk, wearing a determined and eager expression, was a plucky eighth grader in round glasses and butterfly barrettes.

"Good news, Mr. Ferrars," Bethesda Fielding announced confidently. "I am going to find that trophy!"

For the first time that day—for the first time in what felt like years—Jasper smiled.

"Well, then. How can I help?"

5

Three Little Letters

Exactly six and a half minutes later, Bethesda stood at the Achievement Alcove, her Semi-Official Crime-Solving Notebook clutched to her chest, while Janitor Steve read the note from Mr. Ferrars.

"All right," he said at last, shrugging. "Looks good to me."

And just like that, the guardian of the crime scene stepped aside and gestured Bethesda Fielding in. Having the assistant principal as her man on the inside was already working its magic.

Bethesda had been in the Achievement Alcove plenty of times before, of course. It was a nook, five feet by five feet square, recessed off the Front Hall just a few steps from the door to the Main Office. The Achievement

Alcove was where the triumphs and successes of the student body, no matter how small, were proudly displayed. The walls of the alcove, as always, were decorated with all sorts of congratulatory posters: there was Marisol's charcoal drawing of a fruit bowl, which Ms. Pinn-Darvish had given a prize, calling it the best student work she'd ever seen; there was a perfect-attendance citation for a seventh grader named Milo Feldberg; there was a congratulatory note to Coach Vasouvian, for three years and counting of no one getting concussions in gym class.

And there, standing in the center of the alcove, was Mary Todd Lincoln's first-ever trophy-display case, which had been hastily constructed by Mr. Wolcott's Industrial Arts class on Monday morning, specifically to house Pamela's trophy. It was a wobbly wooden stand, topped by a tall, rectangular glass cabinet. The glass case bore a jagged hole where the trophy thief had smashed it.

Bethesda examined the case and narrowed her eyes. Something was wrong.

"Wait. What happened to the glass?" she asked.

"All swept up, kiddo," answered Janitor Steve. He was leaning against the wall just outside the alcove, for some reason tapping his broom handle insistently against the air duct that ran along the ceiling of the Front Hall. "Principal told me to leave everything how it was, and I did, to a point. Maybe Janitor Mike, over at Grover Cleveland Middle School, would stand for a bunch of glass all over the floor, but not me."

"Gotcha." She turned to the Alcove, but Janitor Steve stopped her.

"Hey. Kid. You hear anything weird in this duct?"

"Sorry?"

"Anything kinda unusual?" He peered up at the air duct, scratching his neck. "Like little noises or something?"

"No," said Bethesda, impatiently, ready to get to work. "No, I don't hear anything."

"Yeah," he said. "Yeah, me neither. Forget it."

The custodian lowered his broom and leaned against the wall, and Bethesda at last got going. On her hands and knees she crawled methodically through the Achievement Alcove, inch by inch, hunting for clues. After what felt like an eternity of careful searching, across the floor of the alcove and up and down and inside the broken trophy case, Bethesda's jeans were covered with bits of fuzz and dirt, her back ached, and her eyes felt all pinchy from squinting.

She looked at her watch, a gift from Tenny Boyer; like Tenny's bedroom clock, it featured a picture of Pete Townshend, the legendary guitarist from The Who, executing his signature windmill guitar maneuver. Sadly, Pete's hands told her that time was almost up; even more sadly, the Sock-Snow notebook contained a pathetic two clues.

Clue #1. The drops of blood

Bethesda couldn't say for sure they were drops of blood. But they were definitely bloodred, the eleven little red blotches she had discovered staining the glass of the case, all around the hole where it had been smashed. These minute drips, red and long dry, actually looked like they could have been left by cherry cough syrup, or a strawberry lollipop. But somehow "cough syrup stain" or "lollipop residue" wouldn't look as cool in a semi-official crime-solving notebook as "drops of blood."

Clue #2. The teeny tiny screw

Bethesda had a strong suspicion that this wasn't really a clue at all. The little screw probably had tumbled from somebody's overstuffed pocket, or taken a ride to school in the treads of a sneaker. But it was way too early in her investigation to discount any possible clue too hastily. So the teeny screw went into her eyeglasses case for safekeeping, and was duly recorded in the Semi-Official Crime-Solving Notebook.

Two clues. Not the most promising start to her investigation. Bethesda shouldered her backpack, nodded to Janitor Steve, and then turned to take one last look at the crime scene.

Her jaw dropped.

The bell rang.

The hallway filled with the bustle and yelp of the post-lunch rush, and suddenly Bethesda had less than five minutes to get to her locker, ditch the Sock-Snow, and grab *The Last Full Measure*, her book of Civil War primary sources, which she would need for Mr. Galloway's sixth period. But she just stood there staring past the shattered trophy case at the three little letters, written in tiny black print on the back wall of the Alcove itself.

She tilted her head, squinting to make out the tiny writing. IOM.

"Bethesda?" warned Violet Kelp, her pigtails bouncing as she raced by. "You do *not* want to be late for Galloway!" But Bethesda ignored her. She stepped back into the alcove, taking one last careful look at this new clue. Was it actually *I zero* M? Was it an upside-down WOI?

Bethesda flipped back open her notebook and scribbled wildly on a fresh page. She punctuated this new piece of evidence with a cluster of exclamation points, like a little forest had sprung up at the end of the sentence.

Clue #3. IOM!!!!!!

Finally, and with great reluctance, Bethesda left the crime scene behind.

6

"Police and Thieves"

That Thursday afternoon, at precisely 4:47 p.m., an unremarkable woman with mousy, shoulder-length brown hair, clad in a simple brown dress, brown sweater, and sensible brown shoes, examined the dusty sleeve of an old LP record and shook her head patiently.

"No, young man. I'm looking for the *first* Clash album. The one with 'Police and Thieves' on it."

"Oh. All right. Hold on a sec, lady." The record store clerk gave the woman a tight-lipped, irritated smile and strolled lazily to the back of the store.

Ida Finkleman flipped through the racks while she waited, pulling out a Jawbox album and running her finger down the track listings, trying to remember if this was the one she had already. The drive to this record store was quite long, and the clerks were preposterously rude, especially considering that Ida was frequently the only customer. But it couldn't be helped. Once upon a time, all Ms. Finkleman listened to was classical music— Tchaikovsky and Haydn, Brahms and Bach, and especially her beloved Mozart. But that was before last semester. Before the Choral Corral and the Careless Errors; before Bethesda Fielding used a project in Mr. Melville's class to dig up her punk rock past and broadcast it to the world.

In the aftermath of these extraordinary events, Ms. Finkleman had, to all outward appearances, returned to her former role in the Mary Todd Lincoln landscape: the boring and unremarkable Band and Chorus teacher, walking briskly through the halls with her head down and her violin case clutched to her chest. Except Ida had not come away unchanged, not really. What she had gained—besides a keen determination to avoid student projects of all kinds—was a newfound passion for rock and roll.

"Say," Ida asked the returning clerk, gesturing to the in-store stereo system. "This is the Flaming Lips, right?"

The clerk grunted in the affirmative and handed her the Clash album she'd asked for.

Ms. Finkleman rarely had a chance to drive all the

way over here and indulge her new obsession; she was not terribly pleased, therefore, to feel the insistent vibration of her cellular phone. She was even less pleased to discover on the other end a nervous female voice she didn't recognize.

"Hello, is that Ida? It's Tracy."

"I'm sorry?"

"Tracy Fischler? From the math department? I'm here with some of the other teachers. Ida, we, uh . . ."

"Yes?" She ran her finger over the record, checking for nicks and scratches. "What?"

"We need your help."

7

Chester Did It!

On Friday morning her trophy had been gone for four days, and Isabel Van Vreeland decided it was time to get serious. It was time, in other words, for some classroom visits. All morning she prowled the hallways, selecting classrooms at random, throwing open their doors and sweeping inside.

"Who stole my trophy?" she hollered, pointing an angry finger at whatever student she found suspicious. "Did you steal it? Did you?" Principal Van Vreeland's criteria for suspiciousness were somewhat nontraditional: for some reason she seemed to distrust really tall children, left-handed children, and those with purple backpacks.

"Was it you?" she demanded, bursting into Ms. Aarndini's Home Ec. room midway through fourth period, violently emptying the purple backpack of a sixth-grade girl named Heather Long.

"Oh dear," said Ms. Aarndini helplessly. "Oh dear."

But the result was the same in Ms. Aarndini's room as it had been in every other room, all morning long. All the children denied it, and Principal Van Vreeland hissed and huffed and finally slammed the door, leaving behind a mightily flustered Ms. Aarndini and a room full of rattled, restless students, their hands trembling too much to safely use craft scissors.

"Why can't I simply seize these children and shake them by the lapels until they confess!" she demanded of poor Jasper, who raced down the hall at her heels, barely keeping up as she stomped toward another classroom.

"Well—that is—" he stammered. "I don't think children really wear lapels. . . ."

Principal Van Vreeland wasn't listening. She'd already flung open the door to the next room and charged inside, hands cupped around her mouth like a megaphone. *"Who stole my trophy?!"*

As it happened, this next room was Mr. Darlington's. When the door slammed open, with a loud *BAM!*, it so rattled the mild-mannered science teacher that he dropped his sample weather-system diorama, a flood-plain ecosystem, requiring fifteen minutes and a significant deployment of paper towels before class could resume.

By the time the floor was dry and the principal was gone, the period was almost over, and Mr. Darlington was struggling to regain his students' attention. "Children? I know there's a lot going on around here this week. But there's *also* a lot going on in the swirling eddies of a sandstorm. Like, for example—"

BAM! The door swung open and cracked against the wall again. Mr. Darlington jumped and brought a hand up to his chest, while all eyes turned to the doorway.

There stood Suzie Schwartz, Shelly's identical twin sister, clutching a bathroom pass. Suzie's eyes were wide with excitement behind the neon pink, non-prescription glasses she had recently started wearing to distinguish herself from Shelly. "It was *Chester*! Chester Hu stole the trophy! He's going to the principal to confess right now! Can you believe it? I can't even believe it. Hey, Shelly! Got to go. 'Bye!"

She slammed the door shut behind her.

"Chester?" said Rory.

"Chester *Hu?*" said Carmine Lopez.

The ensuing chaos was far too much for Mr. Darlington to even try to control. A confession! The punishment was over! Taproot Valley was back!

Only Bethesda remained quiet, her brow furrowed pensively behind her glasses. Something wasn't right. Chester? *Really?* An idea began to flash in her mind, blinking on and off like a neon exclamation point. For a long minute she tuned out the babble of the room, nodding her head rhythmically, connecting dots, tapping her sneaker on the floor beneath her desk.

"Right," Bethesda said to herself. "That's right."

Then she raised her hand and, speaking loudly to cut through the noise, asked Mr. Darlington if she could go to the bathroom.

"That's fine, Bethesda," he answered as she pushed back her chair and jumped out of her seat. "Although, you know, class is—"

BAM! The door slammed against the wall again, and Bethesda raced out. Mr. Darlington exhaled weakly.

"Class is nearly over anyway."

8

Just in Time

Bethesda raced down Hallway B, rounded the corner, and sighed with relief: There he was.

"Skabimple," Bethesda whispered, borrowing a favorite made-up expression of her father's. ("Skabimple" meant "this could have been bad, but it's good." It was Bethesda's dad's second-most-used made-up expression, after the perennial favorite for expressing sudden shock or pain, "argle bargle.") There was Chester, standing alone at the big wooden office door with its pane of frosted glass, one hand hovering at the knob, eyes closed, psyching himself up to go inside. She had arrived just in time, and now it was up to Bethesda to save Chester from certain doom.

She walked toward Chester slowly, gingerly, almost on tippy-toes, like a nature documentarian approaching a herd of easily spooked zebra. "I have a confession to make," Chester was muttering to himself. "I have a confession to make."

He's practicing, Bethesda thought.

Edging closer, she spoke softly but firmly. "Don't do it, Chester."

"What?" He jerked suddenly and wheeled around. "Oh, Bethesda. Hey."

Chester Hu was a thin, wiry kid with choppy black hair that went off in every direction. His default facial expression was a kind of nervous goofiness, but today the proportions were out of whack: He looked about 80 percent nervous, 20 percent goofy. A little bead of sweat sat on the bridge of Chester's nose.

"Don't open that door," Bethesda commanded, taking another step closer.

A halfhearted grin quickly appeared and disappeared on Chester's face. "I just have to talk to Principal Van Vreeland about Pam's trophy." Chester leaned with comically fake casualness against the door frame.

"But why? You didn't steal it."

"Actually, yeah. I did. So, you know. Gotta confess or whatever." Chester's nervousness/goofiness proportion turned itself up to about ninety/ten.

"Oh yeah?" she asked. "So where is it?"

"I, uh." He looked around helplessly. "I sold it. To some guys."

"Oh yeah?" Bethesda said again. "What did they look like?"

"Um . . . one of them was missing an arm. And the other one was really tall. I think, like, nine feet tall." Bethesda felt like she could actually see Chester's brain working. "I mean, eight feet tall. Seven and a half?"

"Come on, Chester," Bethesda said. "It's really sweet that you want to save the Taproot Valley trip for Marisol Pierce. But you didn't do it."

Chester turned red, as quickly and as completely as if someone had splashed paint on him. "What?!" he protested. "For Marisol? What? That's crazy talk, Bethesda."

He turned away, developing a sudden and consuming interest in the flyers posted outside the office door. "Wow, look at that," said Chester, pointing randomly at an ad for a community theater production of *The Mikado*, featuring Assistant Principal Ferrars in the role of Ko-ko. "Performances at four and seven every day! How 'bout that?"

Bethesda shot a look at her watch. Pete Townshend's

windmilling hands informed Bethesda she only had a couple minutes left before the hallway flooded with kids and Chester got spooked and bolted into the office . . . toward certain doom.

"Look," she said. "Chester, if you confess to this crime, you are going to be in Big Trouble. Serious, Permanent-Record Big Trouble. And Principal Van Vreeland might not give us back the Taproot Valley trip, anyway! You know her. She might leave it canceled, to teach us all a lesson or something. Then what?"

Chester considered this, nodding, his eyes darting worriedly from *The Mikado* flyer to Bethesda and back again.

"And look, if you want to show Marisol you like her . . ." Bethesda paused. Now she was the one blushing; she could feel the warmth creeping up her neck toward her face. This was *so* not her area of expertise. "Just write her a note or something."

"A note?" Chester barked a high, embarrassed laugh. "Have you seen my handwriting? Dr. Capshaw says it's like an orangutan's. Who wants to get a crush note from an orangutan? Besides another orangutan, I mean."

By now, Chester was moving away from the office door. Very carefully, making no sudden movements,

Bethesda guided him back toward Hallway B, and Chester allowed himself to be guided, even as he continued his embarrassed denials. "I mean, even if I did have a crush. Which I don't. Seriously. Orangutans are so funny, don't you think?"

Bethesda had saved the day, and just in time. The bell rang, ending fourth period and sending a torrent of rambunctious kids spilling into the halls, diving for their lockers, grabbing lunch bags, loudly discussing the day so far. As Bethesda and Chester made their way up the back stairs to the eighth-grade lockers, she felt a warm, prideful glow in her chest. It wasn't so long ago that she'd faced serious, Permanent-Record Big Trouble of her own, after the debacle with Mr. Melville's Floating Midterm and the Choral Corral. She knew how it felt to sit on that long bench outside Principal Van Vreeland's office, knew the nauseating gut-terror of impending doom. And now she had rescued Chester from the same fate, and for something he didn't even do!

Never did Bethesda suspect that a day would come, in the not-too-distant future, when she'd wish she'd let Chester make his fake confession after all.

9

All This Trophy Nonsense

As Bethesda guided Chester away from the Main Office, Ms. Finkleman walked toward it, dreading the job she had foolishly agreed to do.

Hers was a ridiculous and utterly useless mission, one that everyone else on the faculty was either too scared or too smart to attempt. Ask Principal Van Vreeland to change her mind? Ms. Finkleman chuckled mirthlessly as she turned the corner into the Front Hall. Principal Van Vreeland *never* changed her mind. Once, when she accidentally had typed three a.m. instead of p.m. in an all-faculty email, the principal had refused to admit her error, and they'd all had to attend a two-hour curriculum-planning meeting in the middle of the night.

Besides, Ms. Finkleman had really hoped not to get involved in all this trophy nonsense. She had so much on her plate already. There was the sixth-grade winter concert—"A Big Boatload of Bernstein!"—she had to prepare. There was the eighth-grade student she was privately mentoring. And there was her seventh-grade Music Fundamentals class, who of course were clamoring to do rock and roll like last year's kids.

But the other teachers had begged her to go ask Principal Van Vreeland to give the kids their extracurriculars back, so everything could return to normal. "She respects you," Ms. Fischler had argued. "I mean, after the whole thing with the Choral Corral, she didn't kill you."

That seemed like a pretty low standard for respect to Ms. Finkleman, and yet here she was, slowly pulling open the door of the Main Office. And there was her elegantly dressed, agitated boss, perched on the edge of Mrs. Gingertee's desk, reviewing student records with the help of the cowering assistant principal.

"Principal Van Vreeland?" Ms. Finkleman ventured. "I—"

"Whatever it is, it can wait!" snapped the principal, waving a folder as if evidence would fly out if she shook it hard enough. "All that matters right now is finding that trophy!"

"That's just it, Principal," Ms. Finkleman began. "The other teachers and I have noted, it somewhat interferes with the educational process—"

"Ms. Finkleman! Please! No time!"

"No time! No time!" echoed Jasper, like a parrot. He gathered up an armful of student folders, and the pair of them disappeared into the principal's private office.

"Well, then," said Ms. Finkleman to the empty air. "Thanks anyway."

She sighed. *What a waste of time.*

But if Ms. Finkleman hadn't been the one to take on the useless mission, she wouldn't have been the one standing outside the Main Office at that moment, turning her head by happenstance toward the Achievement Alcove, directly to her left. She wouldn't, then, have seen the clue—the same three little letters, IOM, written on the back wall beneath Marisol Pierce's fruit-bowl drawing, that Bethesda had seen two days earlier.

But Ms. Finkleman *did* see the clue—and knew immediately, or thought she knew, what it meant.

She was involved in all this trophy nonsense now, like it or not.

✦ ✦ ✦

Bethesda, still enjoying the pleasant sensation of having done Chester a good turn, adjusted her butterfly barrettes in the mirror in her locker, cheerfully saluted her Benjamin Franklin action figure, and grabbed her lunch. A few minutes later she emerged from the school and found her favorite seat at the picnic tables.

On that list of inalienable rights belonging exclusively to eighth graders, eating lunch outside at the picnic tables was very near to the top, second only to the Taproot Valley trip itself. The cluster of sagging, battered tables, arranged in a loose semicircle just to the right of the school's front entrance, was officially open to any Mary Todd Lincoln student who felt like eating there. Unofficially, however, it was eighth-grader territory.

It was a beautiful day, and everyone was outside. Hayley, her retainer resting snugly in its orange case. Shelly Schwartz, with her sister Suzie beside her in the pink-framed glasses. Kevin McKelvey, tall and thin in his rumpled blue blazer, munching an apple and flipping through a thick book of sheet music. Pamela and Natasha, whispering to each other.

But still something . . . Bethesda couldn't put her finger on it, but something was off somehow. Was it just that Todd Spolin, whose interests were traditionally limited to heavy metal music, pro wrestling, and spitballs, was whistling gently to the little blue-green swallow, sweetly offering it bites of his Ding Dong?

Bethesda opened her lunch bag and carefully removed three click-top containers. "Oh, sweet," she said, cracking open the first translucent box. "Spaghetti!" She looked around, prepared for the onslaught of would-be bite-havers. Bethesda's dad's cooking skills were semilegendary among her friends, as was his uncanny ability to arrange even the messiest, most complicated meals into neatly stacked portable containers.

"All right, who wants?" offered Bethesda, waggling a sloppy forkful.

"No thanks," said Shelly, and Suzie remained silent. Hayley, on the far end of the opposite bench, muttered, "Can't," and gestured vaguely to her retainer. Bethesda angled the pasta-laden fork toward Violet Kelp, who shook her head.

"Okay . . ."

This was weird. Violet *always* took a bite, as would anybody who had peanut-butter-and-jelly packed for her every day. But today Violet kept nibbling her sad little sandwich.

"Anybody else going insane about Fischler?" asked Bethesda, raising her voice to reach all four tables. The first big math test of the year was looming, and complaining about it had become a daily routine. But today, no one seemed to be up for a gripe session. Even Braxton, who could usually be relied upon to complain about any subject, at any time, wouldn't meet Bethesda's eye.

"All right," said Bethesda finally. "Shelly? Is something going on?"

Shelly sighed and laid a firm hand on Bethesda's shoulder. "Okay. Well, it's not a big deal, but people are kind of mad at you."

"Really?" Bethesda swept her gaze anxiously around the tables again. Like most people in the universe, Bethesda liked to think she didn't care when people were mad at her; also like most people in the universe, she actually cared a lot. "Who?"

"Oh, you know . . . ," Shelly began, then glanced pleadingly at Suzie, who reluctantly finished the thought: "Everybody."

A small twisted leaf came unstuck from the oak and drifted down into Bethesda's open container of spaghetti, but she ignored it.

"What are you talking about?"

"Well, Violet said that Ellis said Lindsey Deming saw you talking to Chester, when he was right about to go in and confess, and that you stopped him."

"So?"

Shelly and Suzie looked at each other, shaking their heads. "It's *Taproot Valley*, Bethesda."

"I know. But—"

Violet put down her sandwich and chimed in. "It's so obvious. You want to solve the mystery yourself, so you stopped Chester from confessing, which would have saved the trip."

"Just so you can be the one to figure it out," added Suzie. "And be like this big hero, or whatever."

"That's crazy, you guys," Bethesda protested. She raised her voice. "I mean, Chester is innocent."

"Maybe," answered Ezra. "How do you even know?"

"Because . . . well . . ." Bethesda's nervous fingers clacked and unclacked the lid of her smallest lunch container, which held three miraculously crisp pieces of garlic bread. She did know, but explaining would mean betraying Chester's crush on Marisol. "I dunno," she said, feeling impossibly lame. "I just do."

It hadn't really occurred to her that the others would

be so disappointed. Yes, everyone wanted to go to Taproot Valley, but surely a week of ropes courses wasn't as important as truth! And justice! And all that kind of stuff!

"Now listen up, people!" Bethesda said forcefully. Suzie, Shelly, and Hayley stopped eating. Todd Spolin looked up as the bird flew off with a morsel of Ding Dong clutched in its beak. Everybody waited, staring at Bethesda: Marisol Pierce, her face cradled glumly in her hands; Braxton, slurping noisily from a Capri Sun; Pamela, her blue eyes bright and skeptical beneath her perfect blond eyebrows.

"I'm *going* to solve the mystery," Bethesda proclaimed, looking from picnic bench to picnic bench, summoning her most confident and convincing lawyer-lady voice. "I'll figure out who did it, get Pamela's trophy back, and our trip will be saved!"

"Okay," said Suzie. "I hope so." Rory muttered something Bethesda couldn't quite hear, but it sounded like "you better." Only Todd, of all people, offered something approaching support.

"Don't worry about it, dude," he said. Todd, Pamela's second-best friend after Natasha, had long, stringy brown hair and wore a battered old baseball cap every single day. "Maybe this whole trophy thing isn't that big a deal."

Pamela tilted her head, narrowed her eyes, and swiveled toward Todd; Natasha repeated each gesture a split second later. "What do you mean, *not that big a deal?*"

"I don't know." He shoved the rest of his Ding Dong in his mouth, crumpled up the bag, and tossed it in the trash. "Whatever."

Pamela and Natasha shook their heads and turned their backs to Todd. Everyone else went back to their lunches—except Bethesda. No longer all that hungry, she grabbed her backpack and walked inside. Fleetingly she wished Tenny Boyer was still here; in a roundabout way, he had become her closest friend last year, before transferring to St. Francis Xavier Young Men's Education and Socialization Academy. Tenny was mumbly and tended to get distracted and space out in the middle of conversations, but he would never shut her out like this.

But Tenny wasn't here. She was on her own.

Well, Bethesda thought, *I wanted to solve the mystery. Now I have to.*

10

A Bang and Then a Crash

A few hours later, after the seventh-period bell and the mad rush that marked the end of the school week, Ms. Finkleman ushered an eighth-grade girl named Reenie Maslow into the Band and Chorus room. She offered Reenie a seat across from her and a clementine orange from the bowl on her desk. Reenie took the seat, carefully placing her backpack on the ground beside her, but politely declined the fruit. Reenie was a short, delicate-featured girl with dark red hair and glasses, and at this moment she was looking just a little bit puzzled. This puzzlement was something Ms. Finkleman could well understand. If Reenie *wasn't* the guilty party, then she must be wondering what she was doing in the Band and Chorus room for a one-on-one after-school "talk." And if she *was* guilty, she must be wondering why the school music teacher was the one interrogating her about it.

"So, Reenie," Ms. Finkleman began tentatively. "How has your experience at Mary Todd Lincoln been thus far?"

"Fine, I guess." Reenie paused, shrugged. "It's nice here."

Ms. Finkleman nodded. "Good, good."

Reenie sat politely, looking more puzzled by the second. Ms. Finkleman sighed and shifted uncomfortably on her chair, thinking of various places she'd rather be: browsing at the record store; at home drinking tea, listening to Chopin's waltzes.

Okay, Ida, she chastised herself. *Let's get this over with, shall we?*

"Reenie, did you steal Pamela Preston's gymnastics trophy?"

Bethesda was halfway down Hallway B, bicycle helmet already on, Semi-Official Crime-Solving Notebook tucked under one arm, ready to be stowed in her bike basket. She was going to stop at the Wilkersholm Memorial Public Library to research a couple questions, maybe check out some of her favorite mysteries again, to read over the weekend for inspiration. With the whole eighth grade now officially expecting a solution, it was time to kick this investigation into high gear.

"Psssst! Bethesda!"

In the doorway of the art room, a dark figure was beckoning her with one crooked finger.

"Ms. Pinn-Darvish?"

"Step in for a moment, young lady. We need to talk."

Pale, raven-haired Ms. Pinn-Darvish stepped aside with a dramatic flourish as Bethesda entered her domain. The art room had an odd smell, sweet and chemical, a mixture of acrylic paint, paste, and the ginger-scented candles that Ms. Pinn-Darvish was now unloading from a shoebox. Bethesda perched on one of the tottering stools that lined the art room's long rectangular tables. Some kids liked to say Ms. Pinn-Darvish was a witch, but Bethesda knew that was silly; she was just witch*like*.

"So . . . ," Bethesda began, intrigued.

"Patience. Patience," whispered Ms. Pinn-Darvish. "Let me just finish setting up my candles."

If Ms. Pinn-Darvish was getting candles ready, it meant that Monday they'd be having Slide Day. This was a semi-occasional feature of Ms. Pinn-Darvish's class that was bizarre and fascinating the first time, and pretty boring every time thereafter. On Slide Day, students didn't make art, they *looked at* art, and *thought about* art. As Ms. Pinn-Darvish liked to say, they *communed with* art. To facilitate that mystical communion, Ms. Pinn-Darvish would light candles, dim the overhead halogens, and project famous paintings from her computer onto the side wall of the room, while electronic music gurgled from the small black stereo in the corner of the room.

"Bethesda," Ms. Pinn-Darvish began as she set out the candles in little clusters, one cluster per table. "I understand you're trying to solve the Mystery of the Purloined Statuette."

Ooh, thought Bethesda. *Purloined Statuette sounds a lot cooler than Missing Trophy.*

"This unfortunate incident occurred on Monday, did it not?"

"Yes," Bethesda confirmed. She took off her bike helmet, stuck it on the table, and opened the Sock-Snow. Was Ms. Pinn-Darvish, of all people, about to provide her with a crucial clue? She breathed deeply, and the ginger scent of the unlit candles filled her nose.

"On Monday evening, I was walking past the school." Ms. Pinn-Darvish made a final adjustment to the last grouping of candles and settled on a stool across from

Bethesda, her hands steepled before her.

"Monday evening? What time?"

Ms. Pinn-Darvish twisted up her mouth and tilted her head back and forth, thinking.

"About five forty-five, I suppose. That's when I walk Tiberius."

"Tiberius is your dog?"

"*Dog*? No. Tiberius is a potbellied pig."

"You have a pet pig?"

"In a way, young lady, I am his pet, as much as he is mine."

"Okay . . . so . . ."

"Our walk was disturbed by a noise. A loud noise. A *bang* kind of a noise."

The glass! Bethesda thought. *Ms. Pinn-Darvish heard the breaking glass of the trophy case! Except . . .*

"Wait. More like a *crash*, right?"

"Well, that's the odd thing, you see. There *was* a crash, but it came a second later. The bang came first, and *that's* what startled Tiberius. Poor little fellow was quite confused."

A crowd of thoughts jostled for space in Bethesda's mind.

She thought: *A bang, and then a crash?*

She thought: *Did anyone* else *hear that bang?*

She thought: *How do you know when a potbellied pig is confused?*

A little before four o'clock, Janitor Steve yawned a big, long, end-of-the-week yawn and resumed his slow progress down the Front Hall. He was pushing his extrawide bristly broom and his gigantic rolling trash can, gathering up dust balls and crumpled-up late passes and granola-bar wrappers from his beautiful floor. Bending to pick up one tattered sheet of loose-leaf, he saw that it was decorated with a not-half-bad cartoon of Principal Van Vreeland, shouting and waving two stick-figure fists in the air.

"Heh heh," said Janitor Steve, and then jerked nervously at the sound of footsteps coming down the hallway. But no—it wasn't the clack of Van Vreeland's heels, but the squeak of sneakers on linoleum. It was that bubbly kid with the glasses, Bethesda, the mystery solver, hurrying from Hallway B toward the front door, her head bent down, scribbling furiously in a notebook. Janitor Steve had barely resumed his sweeping when another student—a new girl, Irene or something— stormed down Hallway C and swept past him like a fast-moving thundercloud.

And then, just as the door slammed behind her, along came Ms. Finkleman, the music lady, looking exhausted. She nodded politely, like always, and pushed open the front door.

Now that he was reasonably sure the school was empty, Janitor Steve lifted his broom handle and tapped on the air ducts, just as Bethesda had seen him do on Wednesday, when she came to investigate the Achievement Alcove. He tapped, and then listened— tapped again—nothing. Last week the vents had been making strange noises, noises that had kept Janitor Steve on edge: little pops and pings and bangs. Now, though, nothing.

"You got what you wanted, didn't you?" he said, peering up at the silent ducts. "You got what you wanted and now you're gone."

He knew. Janitor Steve knew exactly who had stolen that trophy, and he knew why. But nobody had bothered to ask.

11

Take That, Freakazoid!

It was Bethesda's habit, when she needed the internet, to use the computers at the library. They had a computer at home, of course, in her father's messy den, but Bethesda preferred the library computers, because (A) they were a heck of a lot faster, and (B) when she was on the library computers, her father wasn't standing behind her, telling her the fascinating origin of the term "mouse pad" for the seven hundredth time.

Unfortunately, only one of the library computers was working, and a wide-eyed fourth grader in a plaid button-down shirt and headphones was immersed in some sort of outer-space alien-shooting game, bouncing crazily in his seat, whispering, "Take that, freakazoid!" over and over. Bethesda put her name on the sign-up sheet, and was heading to the detective fiction section to kill some time when she saw Reenie Maslow.

"Oh. Hey, Reenie," said Bethesda in a quiet library voice. She gave a little wave as she walked over to the beanbag chair where Reenie was settled, a book balanced on her lap, one finger idly twisting her hair. "What are you doing here?"

Reenie looked up and scowled fiercely, and Bethesda stopped. All she had meant by "What are you doing here?" was just "Why are you at the library today?" Nobody came to the library on Friday afternoons—nobody but Bethesda, anyway. But Reenie clearly thought she meant "What are *you* doing here?," as in "You don't belong here." Reenie didn't answer, just made a kind of irritated noise in the back of her throat and went back to her book.

Argle bargle!

Bethesda had tried over and over to be friendly to Reenie Maslow, just as she tried to be friendly with all new kids. But Reenie always seemed to take things the wrong way, always seemed to be actively seeking out reasons to be annoyed. It was especially frustrating because, in theory, Bethesda and Reenie Maslow should have gotten along great.

Fact: they were both short.

Fact: they both had tannish-reddish hair that they wore pulled back, Bethesda in barrettes or a pair of short pigtails, Reenie clipped above her ears.

Fact: they both liked to read. Her whole life, Bethesda had never known anyone who liked books as much as she did, a fact she had always taken secret pride in. Back in elementary school, Mrs. Levine had posted a reading chart, on which each completed book earned you a new sticker. Eventually she had to staple an extra strip of poster board at the end of Bethesda's row, which poked haphazardly off the side of the chart, overladen with stickers like a bent, snow-covered tree limb. But Reenie was even more of a bookworm than Bethesda; every time you saw her, her backpack was bulging with books.

So they *should* have been friends: two short, book-loving, glasses-wearing girls with reddish hair. And yet . . .

"Hey, what are you reading?"

Reenie looked up at Bethesda, exhaled with impatience, and said, "A book, okay?" Then she looked back down, exaggeratedly flipped to the next page, and kept reading.

"Bethesda?" called the librarian, Ms. Gotwals, from the computer desk. "Bethesda Fielding?"

Thank god. It was four fifteen, the alien-slaying fourth grader was forced to relinquish his seat at the computers, and Bethesda had an excuse to escape this awkward non-conversation. She settled into the hard plastic chair, flipped open her Sock-Snow, and commenced her research. In half an hour she filled her notebook with all sorts of brilliant mystery-solving advice. She found tips on making timelines, tips on evaluating evidence, and (best of all) tips on what one website called the "classic physiological signs of guilt": sweating, shaking, eyes darting around the room, long pauses in speech. . . .

And then, too soon, it was four forty-five, and Bethesda had to give the computer back to the fourth grader, who was waiting anxiously to reclaim it. She was strapping on her bike helmet, getting ready to go, when Bethesda's eyes landed again on the small, thin figure of Reenie Maslow, lost in the smooshy heap of the beanbag chair, her legs tucked beneath her, immersed in what she was reading. The pose of book-loving absorption was so familiar, Bethesda felt like she could be looking in a mirror.

Should she try to talk to Reenie again? She heard her father in her head, gently encouraging her to try. *Resentment is the worst tasting mint of all,* he'd say.

It takes more muscles to frown. Only you can prevent forest fires. (Or whatever.)

"I'll see ya round, Reenie."

"'Bye," Reenie answered, and flashed a quick, half-friendly smile before bending back to her book. *Well*, Bethesda thought, *it's a start. Now what?*

"Oh, hey, Reenie, random question for you," Bethesda said. "You weren't by any chance hanging around school on Monday evening, were you?"

Reenie tensed, slammed the book closed, and glared at Bethesda. "No! God! Why would you even accuse me of something like that?"

"Accuse you? No! I wasn't! Reenie . . ."

Too late. Reenie Maslow heaved herself up out of her beanbag chair, grabbed her bag, and stomped out of the library.

"I didn't mean it like that," Bethesda protested helplessly, but no one was listening. Ms. Gotwals was away from her desk, the boy at the computer was immersed in freakazoid destruction, and Reenie Maslow was long gone.

Bethesda left the library, unchained her bike, and pedaled slowly home.

12

"1952 Vincent Black Lightning"

The next day was a perfect autumn Saturday, cool but not cold, where the whole world smells like crisp leaves and warm apple cider. It was the kind of day that says, "Hey! Kid! Grab a ball of some kind and get out here! Enjoy the day!"

But Tenny Boyer was in his windowless basement, playing guitar. He was trying to teach himself a song called "1952 Vincent Black Lightning," by a British singer-songwriter named Richard Thompson, who Tenny had only just recently discovered. The song had lyrics, about this dude with a motorcycle and this girl he falls in love with. Or maybe the dude is in love with the motorcycle. Tenny wasn't totally clear on that—what he dug was the guitar part on "1952 Vincent Black Lightning," and for the last three hours he'd been sitting in the dimly lit unfinished basement, trying to nail it.

He sailed through the first sixteen bars and launched into the first verse. "Says Red Molly to James, that's a fine motor bike . . ."

Usually the basement was where Tenny went when he felt like a jerk after getting in trouble at school—so he'd spent a lot of time down there over the years. Like in fourth grade, he'd forgotten to get off the school bus, and his dad had to go pick him up at the big parking lot where the buses go for the night. Or in sixth grade, when he'd spaced out and dropped a guitar pick in the turtle habitat in Ms. Kuramaswamy's room, and apparently eating guitar picks is really bad for turtles. And of course there was last year, when he and Bethesda Fielding had cheated on Mr. Melville's midterm. Now that was some serious trouble.

". . . a girl could feel special on . . . a girl could feel special . . . *shoot*." His fingers stumbled on the complex arpeggiation and he started over. Tenny wasn't in trouble this afternoon. Today he was basically hiding, holed up in the basement with his guitar, trying to avoid hearing any more news. Lately, Tenny's parents had had a lot of news.

"Hey. Tenny. I have some news for you," his father had said the first time, about three weeks ago, right after the start of the school year.

A couple days later, it was his mother, calling from the kitchen, sounding anxious and upset: "Tennyson? I'm afraid I have some news I need to share with you."

Stupid news.

"Says Red Molly to James, that's a fine motor bike . . . ," he sang, and then bungled the pattern again, and was starting over when a voice bellowed from the top of the stairs.

"Tenny!"

"Uh . . . what?"

"I've been calling for ten minutes."

"What? Oh, sorry, Dad. I was playing guitar."

"No kidding. Wrap it up."

Tenny ran his hands through his unkempt mass of thick brown hair, wishing he could just stay down here forever. Was that so much to ask?

"One sec, Dad. Lemme just—"

"No. Get up here, Ten. We've got some news for you."

Like Tenny, Pamela Preston was indoors on this beautiful autumn day. Unlike him, however, she was enjoying an extraordinarily pleasant afternoon.

"You just order anything you like, now, children. Anything on the menu."

"Thanks, Mom," said Pamela, and smiled at her mother, who smiled back.

They were at Pirate Sam's, a family restaurant at the mall, where her parents had insisted on taking her and her favorite fellow gymnast, Lisa Deckter, after that morning's practice. After the difficult week Pamela had suffered, her parents had declared that she deserved a treat—or, rather, multiple treats. First, lunch with her teammate; then a special trip with her mom to go outlet shopping; then to the movies.

All week long, her parents had been extra-nice, and so had her teachers. Dr. Capshaw even excused her for not reading chapters five through eight of *Animal Farm*.

"After what you've been through," he said. "It's perfectly understandable." (Actually, she'd foregone the reading to watch a marathon of *You're Going to Wear That?*, a TV show where celebrities made fun of regular people's clothes.)

Her father reached over and patted her awkwardly on the shoulder. "Don't forget to leave room for dessert, kids."

"Thanks, Daddy," she said.

"Thanks," said Lisa.

A girl could get used to this, Pamela thought, as their waiter hobbled over in an eye patch and fake peg leg. *I should be a theft victim more often.*

"Arrgh! I'm Cap'n Shark Breath. What can I be gettin' ye lassies to drink?"

Pamela smiled and ordered a Shirley Temple. "Please don't forget the little umbrella," she told Cap'n Shark Breath. Pamela loved little umbrellas.

Lisa ordered a water. If Pamela had been in any mood to notice other people, she might have wondered why the usually talkative Lisa was being so quiet today. She would have been quite interested, indeed, to hear what was going on in Lisa's head as she scanned the list of entrees, from X Marks the Spot Roast to Yo, Ho, Ho and a Basket of Chicken Fingers.

She'll kill me, thought Lisa. *If she ever finds out, she'll kill me.*

13

Boney Bones

"Hey, Mr. Darlington? I'm really sorry."

"Well, I'll always accept an apology," Bethesda's science teacher replied amiably, smiling down at Bethesda from atop a little step stool. "Though I haven't the foggiest idea what you're apologizing for."

Bethesda had found Mr. Darlington in his room on Monday morning before school, hanging up student projects. In his right hand he held a styrofoam ball, spray-painted red, while his left hand was splay-palmed against the wall, to keep the rest of him from tumbling to the ground.

"Remember? Friday?" Bethesda explained. "I kind of raced out of your class, and never came back."

He chuckled. "Ah, right, right. Well, it's been a crazy

time around here. All is forgiven, Bethesda. *Erf!*"

Mr. Darlington slipped on the step stool, did a jerky heel-pivot, and just barely managed to maintain his balance.

"Hand me the tape, would you, Bethesda?"

Bethesda grabbed a roll of duct tape from where it sat on Mr. Darlington's desk alongside eight more colored globes of styrofoam; this year's seventh graders must be doing the solar system unit. Mr. Darlington's teaching philosophy was all about "bringing science to life," which he did via elaborate three-dimensional projects. His students were always making intestinal-tract reproductions out of cooked spaghetti and party balloons, or crafting elaborate construction paper terrains in old shoeboxes. The finished products went up for display in his room, although none of them ever seemed to come *down*—with the result that every available inch of wall space was crammed with a diorama or model of some kind or another. Reigning over this cluttered museum of a classroom was Boney Bones, an ancient plastic anatomy skeleton just inside the door of the room, little pieces of duct tape marking where bits had fallen off and been repaired.

With an unpleasant *scritch*, Mr. Darlington pulled out

a length of tape and stuck the red model planet in place. "There we are!" he cried happily, and climbed carefully down from the step stool, where he seemed surprised to find Bethesda still standing there.

"Oh. Did you need something else?"

"Actually, yeah. Kind of a random question for you. Were you by any chance hanging around after school last Monday?"

Actually, the question wasn't random at all. Mr. Darlington's classroom was at the mouth of Hallway A, close to the big front doors of the school. Bethesda was hoping he had seen or heard something—maybe someone coming in or out—that could be added to her slowly growing list of clues.

"Last Monday? After school? Oh, you mean, because of the . . . because of this whole trophy situation."

"Exactly."

"Right."

Mr. Darlington climbed back up on his step stool, measuring with his hands whether Neptune was going to fit where it was supposed to.

"So, were you here?"

"Um . . . hmm. Was I? Yes. I was."

A grin danced across Bethesda's face, and she forced

herself to recompose her Serious Mystery Solver Expression. "So, did you see or hear anything out of the ordinary? Maybe around five forty-five?" That was the time Ms. Pinn-Darvish was out walking her dog . . . pig . . . whatever.

For a full thirty seconds, Mr. Darlington said nothing. First he stared out the window. Then he took his glasses off and put them on again, and then he climbed off the step stool and settled behind his desk.

"Mr. Darlington?"

Finally, the science teacher cleared his throat and spoke very quickly.

"Sorry, Bethesda. I was only here till four."

"Four?" Bethesda's heart sank.

"Yes, four at the latest. I stayed after school to pack up my robot, which took about an hour. So, yes, I'd say I was gone by four. And since I don't have a key, of course, once I was gone, I couldn't come back in."

Shoot. If Mr. Darlington was gone by four, he couldn't have seen anyone smashing any trophy cases at five forty-five.

"Your robot?" Bethesda asked anyway; if someone says they have a robot, you sort of have to follow up. But Bethesda only half-listened to Mr. Darlington's explanation, taking a few perfunctory notes in the Sock-Snow. He and his sixth graders had been constructing a mechanical person named Mary Bot Lincoln: "the world's first pencil-sharpening, can-opening, weather-predicting person-shaped classroom companion," as he proudly described her. Last week, Principal Van Vreeland had granted Mr. Darlington's request that Mary Bot, once finished, could be displayed in the Achievement Alcove.

"But last Monday morning, Principal Van Vreeland changed her mind." Mr. Darlington sighed. "She told me that now that space would be used to display Pamela's trophy. So I was here after school, taking the old girl apart."

For one confused moment, Bethesda looked up sharply, thinking Mr. Darlington had been taking Principal Van Vreeland apart. Now *that* would have been a mystery.

"Señoritas? Por favor?"

Third period on Mondays meant Spanish with Señorita Tutwiler; she was slowly circulating through the room, trying to keep her *estudiantes* focused on their two-paragraph translations. But, as was par for the course these days, people had other things on their minds.

"So," said a girl named Lindsey Deming, inching forward and whispering to Bethesda in this kind of not-nice-but-pretending-to-be-nice voice she had, "How's the mystery-solving going, Nancy Drew?" Bethesda whispered back, "Har-dee-har," but the kids sitting around them totally cracked up—including, Bethesda noticed with irritation, Reenie Maslow.

"Come on, guys. She's just trying to help. Right, Sherlock?" said Pamela innocently, with a sly little grin. "I mean, Bethesda."

"I—"

"Bethesda! Pamela! Please!" clucked Señorita Tutwiler, hands planted on her hips. Bethesda mumbled, "Sorry," but Pamela looked right at the teacher, tilted her head, and as if by magic, summoned tears to tremble in her eyes.

"I'm really, really sorry," she said in a quavering voice. "It's just that I'm still so upset about my trophy. . . ."

Señorita Tutwiler half-closed her eyes and raised a hand to her heart, the very picture of sympathy. *"No te preocupes,"* she said soothingly, patting Pamela gently on the cheek. "Never mind."

Oh, come on! thought Bethesda.

✦ ✦ ✦

Bethesda's mood brightened considerably halfway through fourth period. Mr. Darlington was in front of the class, reading from page three of his ridiculously overcomplicated, seven-page instruction sheet for the weather-system project, when it hit her. Bethesda's interview with Mr. Darlington hadn't been a waste of time . . . far from it! She'd gleaned a crucial clue. On Monday morning, Principal Van Vreeland told Mr. Darlington there was no longer any room to display his beloved robot. And why not? Because of the giant trophy that would be taking its place in the Achievement Alcove.

By Monday night, that trophy was gone.

Why, Dr. Watson, don't you see it? Bethesda asked herself in the haughty English accent of Sherlock Holmes. *Mr. Darlington has a motive.*

After science ended, Bethesda decided to stop by the Main Office before lunch to share her intriguing insight with her Man on the Inside. But she forgot about Mr. Darlington, forgot about Jasper, forgot about the robot and the whole thing the moment she opened the office door—because, right beside Mrs. Gingertee's desk, she ran smack-dab into Tenny Boyer.

14

. . . And Better Than Ever

"Hey, dude," said Tenny.

Bethesda never thought she'd be so happy to hear two words, especially when one of them was "dude."

"Tenny!?" she yelped, delightedly pronouncing his name as half exclamation and half question. "What are you *doing* here?"

"Well, you know." Tenny smiled a lopsided smile. "I'm back."

"And better than ever!" Bethesda immediately replied. In Bethesda's family, that's what you said whenever anyone came back from anywhere, whether it was a weeklong business trip, or a trip to the mall. Tenny laughed. "I don't know about that."

"But, I mean—what are you *doing* here?" she said again.

"Well, it's kind of . . . I mean . . . ," he said, and trailed off in a shrug, running a hand through his mess of brown curls. Bethesda spied his iPod earbuds emerging in an ungainly tangle from the blue-hooded sweatshirt he always wore. "It's kind of a long story."

Bethesda beamed at him. Good ol' Tenny Boyer! She had really only gotten to know him halfway through last school year, when they were thrown together by the strange deal Ms. Finkleman had invented to save both the Choral Corral and Tenny's Social Studies grade. That effort had not gone so great, which was how Tenny ended up at St. Francis Xavier Young Men's Education and Socialization Academy.

Except here he was before her very eyes, smiling awkwardly, lifting one foot to scratch the calf of the other with his toe.

Bethesda chucked him on the shoulder. "Well, anyway, who cares *why*. You're back!"

"Ahem," said Mrs. Gingertee. She didn't clear her throat, she actually said the word "ahem," two sharp syllables suggesting that she had more dignity than to go around pretending to clear her throat. "He's not back yet."

She tapped one formidable fingertip on the thick

manila folder, overstuffed with papers, that sat heavily on her desk. "This paperwork is a disaster, young man, and until we've got it straightened out you're no more a student here than my uncle Roger."

"Huh?" said Tenny.

Mrs. Gingertee sighed and pulled out the first of the sheets. "This is the transfer document from St. Francis. Section C is blank, for some reason, and we're missing a signature here, here, and here. . . ."

Bethesda could hardly believe her luck. Tenny was back! The fates had sent her the perfect assistant! This mystery was toast! While Mrs. Gingertee grumbled her way through the paperwork, Bethesda shifted back and forth on her feet, anxious to fill Tenny in on the investigation so far.

"This form is in blue ink. Black is preferable."

"Oh. Okay."

"And this one is in . . . please tell me this isn't colored pencil."

"Oh. Whoops."

Bethesda discreetly eyeballed Mrs. Gingertee's giant metal desk, which was something of an institution at Mary Todd Lincoln Middle School, much like Mrs. Gingertee herself. The desk was a big, battered monolith, half as long as the whole Main Office, of the same rusted-iron color and solidity as a battleship. Only rarely was Mrs. Gingertee spotted anywhere but seated behind it, rolling around in a three-foot radius upon her gun-gray, orthopedically optimized chair. On the desk at present, beside a humongous jar of jellybeans, was a dull green Swingline stapler; a photograph of seven unsmiling grandchildren in matching hideous denim overalls; and papers—lots and lots of papers. Neatly printed sheets, various manila files, tardy slips and excuse letters, beat-up orange interoffice envelopes, and folders of all kinds.

The folder currently open was marked BOYER, TENNYSON ISAAC. Peeking out from beneath it was a second folder, the tab of which Bethesda glimpsed fleetingly as Mrs. Gingertee reached into the Boyer folder for the next form. The name that Bethesda read, upside-down, off the tab, was MASLOW, IRENE OLIVIA.

Bethesda squinched up her face, thinking. Irene? Who was Irene?

Oh. Right. Reenie Maslow.

Irene, Reenie.

Holy Guacamole! Bethesda thought, and then said it—"Holy Guacamole!"—louder than she'd intended, causing Mrs. Gingertee to look up with a sour expression. "Young lady?"

"Sorry, sorry." She exhaled. "But is Tenny almost done?"

Mrs. Gingertee wearily inspected the paper in front of her, flaking crusted pizza sauce off one corner with her fingernail. "I suppose so. For *now*. Tenny, I need you to get this sorted out with your mom or dad for *tomorrow*, okay? Otherwise we can't—hey!"

Bethesda grabbed Tenny by the arm, so forcefully that she nearly toppled him, and together they dashed from the room.

"Come on!" she hollered. "You're never going to believe this!"

Mrs. Gingertee watched the wooden door of the Main Office swing shut, and then produced a bottle of Pepto-Bismol from the top drawer of her enormous desk. "Welcome back, kid," she muttered, and took a long swig.

"Bethesda, what the heck?" said Tenny, just outside the office door.

In one long exhale of a run-on sentence, Bethesda brought Tenny up to speed. She told him about the trophy theft, about the cancellation of the Taproot Valley trip, the tiny screw and the dots of red, the bang and the crash . . . and the *other* clue. Three little letters, inscribed like an artist's signature in one small corner of the crime scene.

"IOM," she concluded, leading him the five feet from the door of the Main Office to the Achievement Alcove. "Right *there*!" She pointed vigorously—and then froze, her face a mask of confusion.

"Um . . . Bethesda?"

She stared in horror at the Achievement Alcove. "It's *gone*!"

Everything else was just as it had been. The cordon of duct tape and typewriter ribbon; the rickety wooden stand and the shattered glass case; the strange, bloodred splotches. All as it had been when Bethesda examined it last Wednesday . . . except for the letters. The letters were gone.

"Huh," said Tenny.

Bethesda slipped under the typewriter ribbon and traced the back wall of the Alcove with her fingers. Maybe it was over here—maybe—wait . . .

"Bethesda? Would you mind joining me in my room for a quick chat?"

Bethesda turned to see Ms. Finkleman, dressed as always in a brown sweater and simple brown shoes, smiling pleasantly. But something in her tone of voice and the slight forward thrust of her chin suggested to Bethesda that this "quick chat" was not a casual invitation from a friend, but a direct order from a teacher.

Bethesda nodded mutely, her mind going a thousand miles an hour. What was going on here?

"Hello, Tennyson," Ms. Finkleman added. "You may as well join us."

15

Another Day, Another Awkward Conversation

Here we go again, Ms. Finkleman thought, as she pulled the door of the music room closed behind her. *Another day, another awkward conversation.*

"Have you children had a chance to eat lunch yet?"

They had not, nor had Tenny brought his lunch, so they pulled up chairs around Ms. Finkleman's desk and Bethesda gave him half of her pasta primavera, the latest of her father's elaborate lunchtime concoctions. Ms. Finkleman additionally offered him a small container of seaweed salad, which Tenny politely but unambiguously declined.

"Dude, it's just like old times. Like a reunion," Tenny announced through a big messy bite of pasta. "Like when the Beatles played on that rooftop."

Ms. Finkleman smiled. She knew exactly what he meant. Here was Tenny Boyer, his cheeks chipmunk-stuffed with pasta, slapping the flats of his hands on his thighs, air-drumming to music only he could hear; and here was Bethesda Fielding, uncapping a Snapple and peering around the Band and Chorus room with that unremitting, intense curiosity of hers.

It *was* kind of nice to be reunited with this particular pair of goofballs.

Enjoy the camaraderie while you can, Ida.

Ms. Finkleman swallowed her first bite of sushi and gave Bethesda the bad news.

"*You* did it?"

"Let me be clear. I did not steal Pamela Preston's gymnastics trophy."

"But you erased the initials?"

"Yes. I did."

Bethesda was flabbergasted. "Why would you do that?"

Ms. Finkleman ignored the question. "Furthermore, Bethesda, I need you to keep the information about the initials to yourself."

"*What?*"

"I'm sorry, but that's just the way it has to be."

Bethesda pushed back a lock of red-brown hair that had fallen over her eyes. "I seriously don't understand," she protested. "I'm trying to solve a mystery here!"

"I know. And all I ask is that you proceed in your investigation as if those initials never existed. The same goes for you, Tennyson."

"Huh? Sure," he said. "I mean, I barely know what you guys are talking about."

Bethesda's confusion, meanwhile, was quickly turning to outrage. This was her investigation! What right did Ms. Finkleman have to order her around? "Hold on a sec. Wait, wait. This is an extremely significant clue." She leaned forward, whispering urgently, trying to make her music teacher see the injustice of her request. "There is only one person in this school with the initials IOM."

"I am aware," Ms. Finkleman replied quietly, rolling slightly forward on the little wheels of her desk chair. "And that's exactly why you're going to ignore them. Reenie Maslow had nothing to do with this crime."

"How do you know that?"

Ms. Finkleman sighed. "I'm sorry, Bethesda. You'll just have to trust me on this."

The music teacher put a piece of California roll in her

mouth and looked away. Bethesda huffed and crossed her arms, shooting Tenny a scowling, "can you *believe* this?" look. But Tenny sat chewing a piece of garlic bread, gazing out the window with a glazed expression that Bethesda knew well; her friend was off in space somewhere, playing a guitar solo at Madison Square Garden or writing lyrics in his head.

Except, when Tenny swallowed his bite and broke his silence, it turned out he was paying attention after all— although what he said irritated Bethesda even further. "Huh. You know, Ms. Finkleman's probably right."

"What?"

"Wait. Just like, think about it. Why would somebody steal something and then sign their name to the crime scene? Don't people who do bad stuff try *not* to get caught?"

"Well yeah, but . . ." But *what?*

"And, I mean, I don't know this Reenie girl," Tenny continued. "But why would she steal someone else's trophy in the first place?"

"Excellent point," said Ms. Finkleman. Bethesda felt outnumbered and a little betrayed. Tenny was supposed to be *her* mystery-solving right-hand man, not Ms. Finkleman's!

"Here's the thing, Bethesda," Ms. Finkleman said softly, laying down her chopsticks in the empty plastic container. "Reenie is new at this school, and my impression is she's not having such an easy time of it."

Bethesda thought of Reenie by herself at lunch with a book propped in her lap; of Reenie sitting perfectly still when Dr. Capshaw announced a group project, while the other kids formed themselves into chatty little teams; of Reenie at the library on Friday, flushed and uncomfortable, overreacting and upset.

"The last thing such a student needs is to be made the subject of a potentially devastating rumor." Ms. Finkleman laid a small but unmistakable emphasis on the word "rumor," and Bethesda blushed. That was one road they'd been down together. "She doesn't need people imagining she's a thief, or the person who single-handedly ruined the eighth-grade class trip."

For all her outrage, Bethesda recognized the soundness of Ms. Finkleman's reasoning. If Reenie *didn't* do it, accusing her would be disastrous. But . . . but . . .

"But Ms. Finkleman. How can you be so sure Reenie Maslow is innocent?"

The Band and Chorus teacher looked Bethesda right in the eye, and for the first time in this whole annoying conversation, Bethesda felt like she was sitting across from the Ms. Finkleman she knew and loved, the sort-of-rock-star Ms. Finkleman, the one who was a human being and treated her students like they were human beings, too.

"Because she told me, Bethesda. And I believe her."

"Well, *that* was weird," Bethesda said, casting a look back at the music room as she and Tenny headed down Hallway C. Tenny didn't answer. He surveyed the halls, a little uncertainly, like an astronaut who'd just arrived on an alien planet.

"This way, Tenny."

"Huh?"

"Our lockers are upstairs this year."

"Oh. Cool."

As they went up Stairway Four, he trailed his fingers on the banister, whistling softly to himself.

"So, it must be kind of fun to be back, huh?" Bethesda asked.

"What? Uh, yeah. I don't know. I guess."

"Speaking of which, I still want to know the story with that," Bethesda said, guiding him to the eighth-grade locker bank. "I mean, what happened at St. Francis Xavier?"

"Well, you know . . . ," Tenny began. "Oh, wait. Here."

He glanced at the locker number Mrs. Gingertee had written for him on a note card. "Twenty-one twelve. Just like the Rush album. Sweet."

"Whatever you say," said Bethesda. She left him wrestling with his combination and sailed off down the hallway toward her own locker.

It was only later, as Bethesda was pulling up her stool at Table Six in the art room for Slide Day, that she realized something: When she came upon them in the Achievement Alcove, Ms. Finkleman had not seemed surprised to see Tenny Boyer. Bethesda hadn't known Tenny was returning to Mary Todd Lincoln, but it sure seemed like Ms. Finkleman had.

Boy, she said to herself, as Ms. Pinn-Darvish lit her ginger candles and cued up the first slide. *This place is just full of mysteries lately.*

16

The Big Warm Fuzzy Mass of Good Idea

"**C**olors . . . so many colors . . . *feel* the colors . . . *experience* the colors . . ."

Chester Hu sank down in his seat and stared at the ceiling. Slide Day wasn't even half over yet. Ms. Pinn-Darvish floated through the room, murmuring about the sublime beauty in the mishmash swirl of colors and shapes currently on display, and occasionally poking kids on the back of the neck to keep them awake.

Chester tugged the collar of his shirt up over his nose to dampen the ginger smell of the candles. He was not a happy camper lately.

First, he'd had the stupidest idea of all time, to march into the principal's office and pretend like he was the one who'd stolen Pamela's trophy. If he'd gone through with it, he probably would have ended up in detention, or expelled, or locked in the basement undergoing some horrible punishment invented by the principal just for him.

But his own stupidity wasn't even what bummed Chester out the most. What really made him mad was how *not*-mad at him everybody was. He had almost saved the Taproot Valley trip, and then, by abruptly changing his mind, he had lost it all over again. But instead of being annoyed at *him*, they were annoyed at Bethesda for making him do it. It's like they thought Chester was too much of a doofus to be responsible for his own actions. Of *course* he would do something crazy like pretend to be the criminal, and of *course* he changed his mind when Bethesda told him to. Blaming Chester would be like blaming a dog for chasing a cat, or a koala for—what did koalas do, again? Eat leaves or something? Chester couldn't remember.

Ms. Pinn-Darvish pressed a button on her computer, and the slide clicked over, from the mushy blur of colors to a field of flowers, waving yellow in the sun.

"*See* the sunflowers," the art teacher intoned, swaying back and forth with her head tilted toward the slide. "*Be* the sunflowers . . ."

And now, Slide Day—the worst way to spend an hour that Chester could imagine, unless it was Thanksgiving dinner at his grandparents' house, watching Grandma Phillis's dentures do battle with a piece of dry turkey breast.

"And now . . . Picasso!" announced Ms. Pinn-Darvish breathlessly, and the sunflower slide gave way to a picture of a hunched, sick-looking dude slumped over a guitar, painted in shades of deep blue and dirty gray.

"Whoa," called out Braxton Lashey, earning a caustic glare from Ms. Pinn-Darvish. "What's wrong with that guy?"

Everyone laughed, except for Chester. He sat up straight and stared deeply, losing himself in the painting, until he felt like he was sitting there beside the wretched figure in that dusty, darkened street. Looking deep into the sad eyes of the guitar man, Chester felt like he knew the guy. This poor sap had probably wanted to be a hero, too, and had probably failed, just like Chester.

"Nobody takes you seriously, either, do they, Mr. Guitar Man?" Chester whispered.

The guitar man turned his head ever so slightly, looked right back at Chester, and *winked*. Later, when he thought about it, Chester was at least half sure he had imagined the wink. But in that moment there was not a doubt in his mind: the shabby blue guitar man had peered from the painting, looked him right in the eyes, and winked.

And just like that, Chester stopped feeling sorry for himself and had the best idea of his life. "Funding for all extracurriculars is being revoked," Principal Van Vreeland had pronounced, pounding on the top of her lectern.

But "funding revoked" is not the same thing as "canceled!" Not the same thing at all!

The good idea sprang into Chester's head with no details, with all the fine points still to be worked out. It was really just a big warm fuzzy mass of good idea. But for Chester, who a minute ago was ready to run home and hide under his bed for a month, that was more than enough. He sat up straight, pointed a finger at the slide, and grinned.

"Nice work, Mr. Guitar Man," he said, and everyone in the room looked at him like he was some sort of lunatic.

Except Ms. Pinn-Darvish. As she clicked the slide from the Blue Period Picasso to a lovely pink-washed Degas ballerina, the black-haired art teacher contemplated Chester Hu with open admiration.

Clearly, Chester was communing with the art.

17

Spleen

On Tuesday morning, Bethesda woke up crazy early and couldn't fall back asleep. She lay in bed squeezing her favorite teddy bear, Ted-Wo (short for the Teddy Bear Who Replaced the One Whose Head Fell Off in the Washing Machine). Every birthday for the last six birthdays, she had declared herself to be too old for Ted-Wo, given him one last kiss, and stashed him in the bottom drawer of her dresser. But somehow or other, he always made it out of the dresser and back into her bed.

"Well, Ted-Wo," Bethesda said in a hushed, early-morning voice. "Who do *you* think stole that trophy?" Ted-Wo was silent on the subject, looking back at her blankly through his one remaining eye. She patted his scraggly fur. "Thanks anyway, pal."

Bethesda gave up on sleep and headed downstairs to make a waffle. Waiting for the toaster oven to *bing*, she thought about Tenny's sudden reappearance, thought about Pamela's little performance in Spanish class, thought about Reenie Maslow and the friendship between them that should have been, but wasn't.

And then she started thinking, for some reason, about Assistant Principal Jasper Ferrars. "*One person* has the key, and *one person* grants access to this building after four o'clock," Principal Van Vreeland had said at the assembly. "And that's this person right here." Mr. Ferrars had gulped and looked nervous, staring down at those overly shined black shoes of his.

Clearly he was scared of Principal Van Vreeland—but was he just scared of her like always, or was he *extra*-scared for some reason? Bethesda buttered her waffle thoughtfully, staring out the window as the sun daubed the backyard in gold and green.

"Tenny? You getting ready up there?"

"Uh—yeah. Totally."

Tenny Boyer was thinking about how to get out of school today. He lay perfectly still, staring at his ceiling, at the spot where three years ago he had written the words

ZEPPELIN RULES with a glow-in-the-dark highlighter pen.

Yeah, it was cool to see Bethesda again, and even a couple of the other kids. And sure, this mystery thing was kind of a trip. But overall?

"Tenny! Five minutes!"

"*Okay*, Dad."

Tenny got out of bed slowly, one foot at a time, and began to dig for something wearable in the crumpled heap of semiclean clothes in the corner of the room.

It wasn't like St. Francis Xavier Young Men's Education and Socialization Academy had been some kind of DisneyWorld. The hallways were always perfectly, scarily clean. The other boys did nothing but work, and half of them had crew cuts. There was this insanely mean math teacher named Father Josef, who in the first week of school gave a kid detention for sneezing. And yet now, as he tugged an R.E.M. concert T-shirt over his unbrushed hair, Tenny would have given anything to go back in time, to three weeks ago; to be, at this very moment, struggling into his St. Francis–mandated striped tie and navy blazer.

Tenny stood at his door and tried to make his voice as thick and wheezy as possible. "Hey, uh, Dad? I'm not feeling—ahem—not feeling so hot."

His father didn't even bother coming up, just yelled from the foot of the stairs. "Oh, yeah? What's the problem?"

"Uh ..." What was a body part that might get messed up in a serious, but impossible-to-detect way? "I think it's my spleen."

There was a split-second pause, and then he heard his father walking from the foot of the stairs back to the kitchen.

"Get dressed, Tenny."

In Mr. Darlington's class that day, the eighth graders were divided into small groups to start their weather-event projects. Usually Bethesda had no trouble finding partners for group work. Just two weeks ago, everyone had wanted to team up with her for the grammar game-show project in Dr. Capshaw's class ("Who Wants to Be an Adverb?"). But today, Suzie and Hayley formed a group with Bessie; Pamela and Natasha offered their last spot to Reenie Maslow, of all people, and Bethesda ended up being one of the only two not picked, paired up by default with the hardworking, studious Victor Glebe.

While they moved their desks around to start working on the project, Bethesda talked to herself.

"He said, 'I don't have a key, of course.'"

"Who?" said Victor.

"But why? Why did he say 'of course'? Why would I think he *does* have a key?" she muttered, glancing at Mr. Darlington as he wandered about the room.

"I don't know what you're talking about." Victor buried his face in their Earth Sciences textbook, carefully copying out relevant statistics. "'Flash floods occur in a timescale of less than six hours.' 'A flash flood is defined as twenty or more inches of rain falling in under an hour.'"

Bethesda nodded, not really listening. And then, somewhere between "worst in areas of arid soil" and "leading cause of deaths associated with thunderstorms," she cracked Mr. Ferrars's secret.

The flyer had said he was appearing in The Mikado *all next week. With performances at four and seven. Which meant . . .*

"Of course! That's it! Perfect!"

Victor Glebe stopped reading and looked at her expressionlessly. "Why would you characterize the deaths of four hundred and sixty-four people in Lisbon, Portugal, in the year 1967 as 'perfect'?"

"Um . . . it's sort of hard to explain."

Victor frowned and lowered his textbook. "Bethesda . . ."

"Sorry, sorry," she said. The last thing Bethesda ever wanted to be was the weak link on a group project! "It's just—"

"I know. The mystery. Which I am *sure* you will solve," Victor gestured impatiently around the class, at the roomful of people all kind-of-mad at Bethesda. "And save the day for us all."

"Aw. Thanks, Victor."

He nodded, once. "Now let's talk floods."

"Everyone? Today we're welcoming a new student—oh, no, sorry, an old student, back again. Heya, Tenny."

According to his new schedule, fourth period on Tuesdays Tenny had Advanced Technology with Mr. Muhammed. (Last year, in Basic Technology, Tenny had earned himself a week of after-school detention for using up a whole toner cartridge printing the guitar tab to "In-A-Gadda-Da-Vida.") He took the laptop that Mr. Muhammed handed him, gave the class a quick smile, and slouched down into a seat, drawing up the hood of his sweatshirt.

As soon as class was over, Tenny turned on his iPod

and popped in the earbuds. He'd created a special playlist last night, full of loud and raucous songs—"Fiesta" by the Pogues, Fugazi's "Waiting Room," a whole bunch of Red Hot Chili Peppers—so he could just totally zone out as he made his way through the halls.

People kept stopping him, anyway.

"Mr. Boyer? Returned to the fold, I see." Mr. Melville planted himself in Tenny's path, his thick white eyebrows raised sarcastically. "Will wonders never cease?"

"What?" Reluctantly, Tenny pressed Pause and took out his earbuds. "Oh. Yeah. Totally."

"Though I suspect I might feel less enthusiastic if I had you in my class." Mr. Melville chortled. Tenny put his music back on.

"Tenny? What's up, man!" hollered Ezra McClellan, intercepting him with a hand raised to slap five. "You back?"

"Uh . . ." Music off. Earbuds out. Five slapped. "Yeah."

"Sweet! So—"

Earbuds back in. Music cranked back up. Out of the corner of his eye Tenny saw Ezra huddle with Tucker Wilson, both of them pointing over at him. Ordinarily the sight, with Tucker so big and Ezra so small, would be comical. But this was exactly the sort of thing Tenny was afraid of, exactly what had made his spleen hurt this morning. Tucker was the kind of kid who was always saying crazy stuff about people. Once he'd told Tenny, in all seriousness, that Lindsey's mother was a CIA agent assigned to keep tabs on Violet's mother, who was an international assassin.

Tenny didn't want to think what Tucker and Ezra, and everyone else, would be saying about him; he had left school, and now he was back, and that would be a subject of conversation, no doubt. Clutching his lunch in its brown paper bag, Tenny Boyer headed for the one place at Mary Todd Lincoln Middle School he knew he'd be totally comfortable: Ms. Finkleman's room.

"Ah! Bethesda!" chirped Mr. Ferrars.

She had found her Man on the Inside in the Main Office, squatting in front of the little refrigerator next to Mrs. Gingertee's desk. "Can I offer you some lunch? I make my own cottage cheese, you know."

"No, thank you," said Bethesda, gesturing at her lunch bag.

"And how is Mary Todd Lincoln's very own private detective getting on thus far?" Mr. Ferrars was so happy to see her, Bethesda knew, because he was the one person in school as desperate as she was for a break in the case. And now she knew why.

"Well, I actually have quite an intriguing lead I'm following today," she said, and he looked up eagerly. "It has to do with you, actually. You and your play."

The assistant principal's knuckles went white, and he slowly closed the door of the little fridge.

"Step this way, won't you?"

18

Nine Keys

"First of all, it is not a 'play.' *The Mikado* is an operetta, and there is a world of difference. Do you understand?"

Bethesda did not understand at all, but nodded as if she did, so he would skip ahead to the good part. The assistant principal sat behind his flimsy wooden desk, twisting his thin fingers anxiously. "I had hoped this wouldn't come up. I really had. Just wishful thinking, really—sheer bootless self-deception. I can't do it, Bethesda! I can't tell her the truth! She'll box me up and ship me off to work somewhere horrible! Like a coal mine! Or an elementary school!"

Bethesda leaned eagerly toward Jasper. "What truth are you talking about, Mr. Ferrars?"

"After-school activities like drama and athletic teams, as you know, have direct access to their respective domains: the auditorium, the gymnasium, or the playing fields. But anyone needing access to the main section of the school is supposed to be let in personally. Principal Van Vreeland leaves every day by three thirty. So who do you think is responsible for letting in all these people?"

"You?"

"*Me*. But I have a life outside these doors, you know! A community-theater production of *The Mikado* is a once-in-a-lifetime opportunity for a bass-baritone such as myself! So for the three weeks of rehearsal and performance, beginning two Fridays ago, I—I . . ."

He paused and took a deep breath. Bethesda remained silent, riveted.

"I took a risk. I made a few copies of the front-door key. Each person given one understood they were to share their key with no one, and to tell no one of its existence."

Mr. Ferrars shifted in his chair, sighing woefully, while Bethesda formulated her next question. "And, okay, so, keys, and so—" *Slow down*, she chided herself. *Put the words in order.* "You said there were a few keys. How many exactly?"

Mr. Ferrars cradled his forehead in his hand and sighed. "Eight."

"Eight keys?"

"Eight keys, including mine."

Mr. Ferrars wouldn't let Bethesda write down the names, but it wasn't hard to memorize the list. The names tumbled about in her head as she left the main office and made her way to her locker.

Guy Ficker
Natasha Belinsky
Lisa Deckter
Pamela Preston
Kevin McKelvey
Ms. Ida Finkleman
Mr. Hank Darlington
Assistant Principal Jasper Ferrars

And then there was Janitor Steve. Jasper hadn't made him a key, but as the school custodian, he carried one on his key ring. A total of nine people, then, had the key. Five kids and four adults. Nine names . . . no! Nine *suspects*. And some of them were already under suspicion. This was *too* exciting!

"Tenny! Hey!"

Perfect timing. Just as she turned down Hallway C, Bethesda spotted her assistant detective emerging from the Band and Chorus room. "I have a major breakthrough!"

"Huh?"

Bethesda plucked the earbuds from Tenny's ears. "A breakthrough? In our mystery?"

"Oh. Right. Totally."

Bethesda paused, the earbuds dangling limply from her hands, while Tenny looked back at her absently. Had he somehow forgotten they were solving a mystery together? As they walked together up the steps to the eighth-grade lockers, and she explained about the keys, Bethesda observed Tenny. She had this strange, troubled feeling, like her old friend was here, but not really. Like even though he had reenrolled at Mary Todd Lincoln, in some weird way Tenny was just as much missing as Pamela Preston's gymnastics trophy.

And what—did he have lunch with Ms. Finkleman every day now?

19

One Song Can Change the World

"Leadership is about three things. Snacks, eye contact, and positive reinforcement."

That's the advice Chester Hu's cousin, Ilene, had emailed him last night. Chester had printed the email, and now he pulled it out—the single page of printer paper a wrinkled mess from having been read and reread all day long—and read it one more time.

As Chester stood beneath the oak tree overhanging the picnic tables, waiting for the others to arrive, he repeated Ilene's mantra to himself: "snacks, eye contact, and positive reinforcement." Ilene was in college, where she was the president of her sorority, vice president of the Association of Premed Students, and the founder of a charity group that fed hungry kittens or something.

Chester's mom was always talking about Ilene, how he should look up to her and ask her questions or whatever. Last night was the first time Chester had actually done so. Ever since he'd had the best idea of his life in Ms. Pinn-Darvish's class on Monday, he'd been alternately superexcited about it and superscared, because doing it right meant putting together a team of people and convincing them to help.

So Chester emailed Ilene and asked for advice. In an extremely supportive two-paragraph reply, above an automatic-signature graphic of an adorable hungry kitten, Ilene explained techniques like "ask, don't insist" and "make it seem like the other person's idea." But really, she said, it all came down to snacks, eye contact, and positive reinforcement.

Which is why, when Rory Daas arrived at the picnic benches a minute later, looking annoyed not to be heading to Game Stop as he usually did on Wednesday afternoons, he immediately said, "Sweet! Snacks!" and plopped down to start eating the Scorchin' Habanero Doritos Chester had provided.

And why when Marisol Pierce slowly walked up, still depressed about Taproot Valley, Chester turned on his best positive-reinforcement voice and said, "Don't even worry about it, Marisol! Everything is going to be fine!" He didn't know if she believed him, but she definitely smiled, and it was the first time anyone had seen Marisol smile since Principal Van Vreeland's announcement.

"Okay, everyone!" chirped Chester, when at last his whole team had arrived. ("Greet everyone enthusiastically," said Ilene's email. "Take charge.") "So, first of all, thanks for coming." As he spoke, Chester scanned the group, looking at each of them in turn.

"What? What is it?" said Natasha suddenly. "Is there something on my face?"

"No, no," Chester apologized. "I was just, um, making eye contact. Sorry."

Rory had another big handful of Doritos. Kevin McKelvey raised his hand. "Chester, is this going to take long? I'm in the middle of learning Mozart's concerto in E-flat. It's kind of a bear." Kevin, also known as the Piano Kid, was Mary Todd Lincoln's resident musical prodigy, who'd been playing sonatas since before he could walk, and spent most afternoons either at home or holed up in the Band and Chorus room, practicing piano.

Pamela Preston's blond curls bobbled slightly as she nodded her agreement with Kevin. "I'm supposed to be meeting Lisa and Bessie in the gym. We have another tournament this weekend. *If* my mother feels the emotional stress won't be too much for me." Pamela sighed dramatically and took a sip from her seltzer bottle, and Natasha squeezed her shoulder.

"Totally understand," said Chester. "I'll try to be quick. I have gathered all of you—Kevin, Suzie, Rory, Pamela, Marisol, Victor, Todd, Natasha, and . . . wait. Braxton, what are you doing here?"

"Oh. Sorry," said Braxton Lashey. "I heard there were going to be snacks."

"Okay, well, stick around, I guess."

And then Chester revealed his plan.

When he was done, to his great relief, no one laughed. No one looked at him like he was stupid or crazy or just a total doofus, not worth listening to. They nodded as he spoke, and asked him questions. Rory stopped eating the snacks, got out a notebook, and started making notes. Braxton took the bowl and ate Scorchin' Habanero Doritos till his hands were stained bright orange, looking up every once in a while to say, "This sounds awesome, man."

And it *did* sound awesome.

First, they would write a song—a beautiful, powerful, heartbreaker of an anthem, about how their outdoor education trip had been cruelly taken away from them. Then they would post that song on the internet, along with a website address where sympathetic people could make monetary donations.

"The thing is, the school only pays for half the trip," Chester concluded. "Our parents already paid for the rest. This group right here, this small but incredibly talented group"—*Positive reinforcement! Positive reinforcement!*— "can, with a single song, earn back the missing money."

"It's a phenomenal idea, Chester," said Kevin. "I love it." Rory, the best creative writer in the eighth grade, was already scribbling song lyrics in his notebook; Marisol, an amazing artist, was doing sketches for the big murals that would be backdrops for some parts of the video. Todd Spolin, who Chester had asked to play guitar in the video, was scrunching up his face, practicing his strained guitar-hero expressions they all remembered from last year's Choral Corral.

"Are you sure a song is best?" asked Pamela, her head angled thoughtfully to one side. "Maybe I should make a dramatic speech instead? I can cry on demand, you know."

"Good thought, Pamela," Chester positive-reinforced. "But I think a song is key. One song can change the world, people. Like 'Happy Birthday.' Just imagine how sad everyone's birthdays were before that."

They set to work, sketching out the song, figuring out details, making a schedule. They decided that the song should start off all soft and tinkly, like it was going to be a ballad or a slow jam, but then turn into a big rock-out. Pamela declared that she would need to be lit from behind, "so my hair looks golden, like gossamer." Suzie ran to check out a laptop from Mr. Muhammed, and by the time Chester finished asking her how long she'd need to build the website, she was done. Rory suggested that for the video to go viral, there would need to be some hilarious part, "like maybe there should be someone in a bear costume who falls down a flight of stairs."

"Ooh! Ooh!" said Braxton enthusiastically. "I'll do that!"

There were only two moments in the entire meeting that interrupted what Ilene's email called the "positive flow." The first came when Natasha, who Chester had put in charge of choreography, said, "Wait, you guys. Tenny Boyer is back. Maybe we should get him to play guitar."

"Perfect," said Chester. But then Todd snorted angrily and sneered at Natasha. "Oh, what, so then I wouldn't be in it anymore?"

"That's not what I meant, Todd," Natasha said.

"So, what *did* you mean?"

"Nothing! *God*, Todd!"

Pamela rolled her eyes. "What is *with* you two, lately?"

Todd muttered, "Forget it," and turned back to helping Rory with his lyrics. This was all very odd: Todd, Natasha, and Pamela were usually supertight, which is part of the reason Chester had invited all three. He decided to skip the Tenny Boyer issue, for the moment.

The *second* moment that interrupted the positive flow, fortunately, didn't come until right at the end of the meeting. They were discussing whether or how to get hold of a smoke cannon for the video's big final moment, when Victor Glebe raised his hand for the first time. Chester grinned as he pointed at him—Victor, after all, was his best friend, and he hadn't said anything so far. He'd just been sitting on the bench farthest from the big tree, arms crossed and face blank, not even eating one of the coconut donuts Chester had brought special for him.

Victor didn't have a suggestion, but a question.

"Do we know exactly how much money it is?" he asked solemnly.

"What?" said Chester.

"To make up what Principal Van Vreeland took away. What's the total?"

"Oh. Uh . . ." Chester fumbled from his pocket a second piece of paper, the one on which Mrs. Gingertee had written down the amount for him. "Four thousand, seven hundred and thirty-six dollars."

"Four thousand, seven hundred and thirty-six dollars," Victor repeated slowly, rising from his seat on the bench. "Four thousand, seven hundred and thirty-six dollars."

"Victor?" Chester said, but his friend was already walking away.

What's his problem? Chester wondered. But there was no time to worry about it now: Marisol was busily sketching for the mural, Rory's notebook was brimming with couplets, and Kevin had already hopped up, ready to head for the old Steinway in the Band and Chorus room.

"All right, folks," Chester said, flashing everyone a big thumbs-up. "Let's do it."

20

World's #1 Principal

The next morning, Principal Isabel Van Vreeland did the same thing she had done every morning since the trophy's disappearance. She stopped on her way to her office to stare, with a mixture of melancholy and horror, into the Achievement Alcove. There it was, the broken glass case atop the rickety wooden stand, where her beloved trophy had ever-so-briefly stood. The longer she stared, the tighter became her grip on her World's #1 Principal travel mug, the one she had bought herself off eBay last year for her birthday.

"Stop right there."

"Oh. Good morning, ma'am."

She turned on Assistant Principal Ferrars, who had literally been tiptoeing past her, clearly hoping she wouldn't ask him what she was about to ask.

"So. How is the mystery solving going?"

His eyes flickered and darted up and down the hall as he stammered a reply. "Oh, you know . . . getting there."

"Getting there?" Principal Van Vreeland squeezed her mug so hard that coffee trembled and spluttered out the top.

He flinched and nodded.

"There's a student helping me. Bethesda Fielding? In the eighth grade? She's quite enterprising, really. She has this, um, special notebook . . ."

"Well, that's fantastic, Jasper," Principal Van Vreeland said, her voice curdling with sarcasm. "Just so long as you've got a twelve-year-old working the case."

As Jasper scurried off, Principal Van Vreeland turned her gaze back into the Achievement Alcove and took a slow, bitter sip from her World's #1 Principal mug. She had a sneaking suspicion that Jasper knew something he wasn't telling her. In fact, she had a sneaking suspicion that a lot of people knew a lot of things they weren't telling her. Instead of helping her get to the bottom of this, and get her precious trophy back, all everyone did was moan and groan about their precious extracurricular activities. Children looked at her all day long with those nauseating puppy-dog eyes of theirs. The teachers had sent that pesty Ms. Finkleman *again* to ask her to change her mind.

Well, guess what, folks. You want me to make things better around here? Too bad. They're about to get a lot worse.

21

"Watching the Detectives"

"So Sergeant Moose says, 'this trail of banana peels can only mean one thing.' And Wellington goes, 'Really, my antlered friend? I think it would *behoove* you to think again!'"

"Dad?"

Bethesda was itching to get to work, but her father had started telling Tenny stories from Wellington Wolf, and once he started it was nearly impossible to get him to stop.

"Get it? He's already be*hooved*! He's a moose!"

"Dad?"

"And it's not Bubbles the Baboon they find, after all. It's Wellington's arch-nemesis, Fiendish Fox, in a *baboon costume*!"

"Whoa," said Tenny, wide-eyed. "That's crazy."

"Yes. Crazy." Bethesda had seen the episode in question (Episode 19, "A Barrel Full of Monkey Business!") and heard her father describe it many times before. Bethesda's father clapped Tenny on the shoulder, sighing with pleasure. "Wellington was right again!"

"Totally," said Tenny. "Though it's sort of like, why would a fox want to rob a bank in the first place?"

"Right," said Bethesda's father, although it was clear from his slightly confused expression that he'd never actually thought of that.

"Dad, we really need to get started."

"I know, pumpkin butter. I'm not bothering you. I'm not even here." Bethesda's father turned back to the gigantic pot of chili on the stove, his latest attempt to perfect his recipe for the charity dinner.

Bethesda hated to be rude, but the Taproot Valley trip was a mere sixteen days away, and they didn't have a moment to waste. For today's crime-solving session, Bethesda had prepared a good selection of supplies: a box of sharpened #2 pencils, an up-to-date map of the school she'd gotten from Mr. Ferrars; and of course the all-important Semi-Official Crime-Solving Notebook (Sock-Snow), which Tenny was now perusing with intense concentration.

"Huh," he murmured, then looked up and said it again. "Huh."

"What?"

"What's this, here?"

"Just my notes from my conversation with Janitor Steve."

"Huh," said Tenny again, reading. "So . . . wait. He said there was glass 'all over the floor'?"

"Yeah."

"Huh," Tenny said a fourth time. He tilted his head back and thought for a long time. So long, in fact, that for a second Bethesda thought maybe he had fallen asleep.

But then he said, "Excuse me? Sir?"

Bethesda's father turned from his stockpot in surprise. "'Sir?'" he repeated, eyes wide with pretended shock. Bethesda was thinking the same thing: *Sir?*

"Do you mind if I fake-punch your microwave?"

Now Bethesda's father looked *really* surprised. "You know, I bet in the whole history of the English language, no one has ever spoken that sentence before."

Tenny was already out of his chair, pushing up one sleeve of his blue-hooded sweatshirt. Bethesda watched, intrigued. What did the microwave have to do with anything? Bethesda's father stepped back, ladle in hand, while Tenny approached the counter, drew back one fist, and gently punched the small appliance in its thick plastic door.

"Ow," he said. But then he punched a second time, slightly harder, and then a third time. Bethesda's father gave a low whistle and said, "Wow. He really hates that microwave."

"Okay, Tenny. What's up?" said Bethesda finally.

"I'm just trying to think logically here, y'know?"

Think logically? Tenny?

What happened to him at St. Francis Xavier? Bethesda marveled. *It's like he's been replaced by some sort of pod person.* But then, the next moment, Tenny absentmindedly picked up a chili-crusted spoon from the counter and scratched his ear with the handle.

Nope, she thought with amused relief. *Still Tenny.*

"The glass of the trophy case was as hard as this on the microwave, right? Maybe even harder?"

Bethesda thought for a second, remembering the little unveiling ceremony, when Mr. Wolcott had set up the glass case built by his sixth-grade Industrial Arts class. "That right there, that's double-paned," Mr. Wolcott had bragged, his thick shop-class goggles dangling around his neck, big sweat stains in full blossom under his arms. "Thickest glass around."

"Harder," said Bethesda. "Way harder."

"Okay, then. So here's observation number one: Our trophy thief would need something a lot harder than a fist to break the glass."

"Smart," Bethesda agreed, and carefully wrote this down on a fresh page of the Sock-Snow, heading it TENNY OBSERVATION #1.

"And here's observation number two. The glass would go in *here*." He opened the door of the microwave and pointed inside. "Not on the *floor.* Right?"

"Yeah," Bethesda said, and then again: "Yeah!" As she wrote TENNY OBSERVATION #2 under the first one, her right foot was squeaking against the linoleum of the kitchen floor. "Of course!"

"Now you're cooking!" interjected Bethesda's father from the stove.

"There might be a *little* glass on the ground, right here around the base," Tenny continued. As if the kitchen cabinet were the trophy case, he traced a tight arc with the toe of his sneaker on the floor. "But not, not . . ." He plucked Bethesda's notebook off the table and flipped back to the interview page. "Not 'all over the floor.'"

"Right! So the question is, what does this mean?"

"Uh, yeah . . ." Tenny shrugged, and slumped back in his chair. "I have no idea."

"But I do!" Bethesda got up and began pacing back and forth across the kitchen. "Our crook smashes the glass and grabs the trophy. But then, for some reason, he pushes all the bits of glass onto the floor." She approached the microwave, pretending to be the thief, acting the whole thing out. "I think he was trying to clean the glass from the case."

"But why?"

"To . . . to . . ." She gasped, and stared intensely at Tenny. "To put something *else* in there!"

"Whoa."

"Whoa," echoed her father.

Tenny scratched his head. "But, uh, then he didn't? Put something else in there?"

"Right."

"I don't know, Bethesda," Tenny said. "What kind of crook would do that?"

Bethesda grinned and lifted her eyebrows. "Excellent question, Watson. Let's talk suspects."

Returning to her seat at the kitchen table, Bethesda unveiled a slim stack of nine index cards, each one bearing a carefully printed name: one card for each person with a key to the building on the Monday when the trophy was stolen, according to Jasper's top-secret list. Each card was a different color, with the suspect's name written in blue ink at the upper-left-hand corner, and Bethesda had three more colored pens at the ready—a red pen for alibi, a green pen for motive, and a purple pen for any additional, miscellaneous information.

"Sweet system," said Tenny, flipping through the cards, and Bethesda grinned. *Let Sherlock Holmes have his magnifying glass*, she thought, arranging the nine cards into a neat three-by-three square. *Bethesda Fielding, Master Detective, has her office supplies.*

"So who's first?" said Tenny.

Bethesda flipped over a card: PAMELA PRESTON, it said.

"Okay, so we can cross her off the list," said Tenny. "It was, like, her trophy, right?"

"Right." But Bethesda hesitated, running the tip of her finger along the edge of the card. She had a theory about Pamela. The theory was probably preposterous, and she definitely wasn't ready to share it. But she wasn't ready to eliminate Pamela as a suspect, either.

"I'm going to keep her in the pile."

"Whatever," said Tenny.

Bethesda and Tenny worked their way through their suspect cards, debating possible motives, passing the Sock-Snow notebook back and forth, laughing at Bethesda's father's occasional Wellington Wolf–related interjections, bouncing wadded-up paper napkins off each other's heads. "Oh! Wait," Tenny said suddenly at one point, and attached his iPod to the stereo with a little cord. He cued up a playlist he'd made of classic crime-solving-related rock and pop songs, from "Watching the Detectives" by Elvis Costello to the ridiculous "Private Eyes" by Hall and Oates.

Some cards they annotated with green for motive, like Mr. Darlington's ("revenge for not being able to display Mary Bot Lincoln") or Guy Ficker's ("mad that Pamela was allowed to use the gym instead of him"). Lisa Deckter's motive was triple-green-underlined: as Bethesda explained to Tenny, Lisa came in second in the gymnastics tournament. Not a bad showing, unless the other competitor from your own team places *first*. Some had purple for alibi: Mr. Ferrars's card, for example, said "was at play practice"; Natasha's said "at Pilverton Mall?," since Bethesda had heard her say she was heading over there to get her nails done after school that day—and

Natasha rarely went to the mall for less than three hours at a time.

Finally, at about 12:30, as Bob Dylan's "Hurricane" segued into Michael Jackson's "Smooth Criminal," Bethesda leaned back and stretched, as Tenny flipped over the last of the suspect cards. It was labeled KEVIN MCKELVEY, but the Piano Kid's card otherwise remained blank. They didn't know if he had an alibi, and neither of them could imagine any motive for mild-mannered Kevin McKelvey to steal a trophy.

"Whoa, I gotta jet," Tenny said suddenly. "Chester Hu asked me to record a guitar solo for some sort of video project he's doing."

Bethesda walked Tenny out to his bike, sprawled haphazardly on the lawn. "Oh, hey, so you never told me what happened," Bethesda said, as Tenny corralled his hair under his silver-black bike helmet decorated with AC/DC stickers.

"What happened with what?"

"At St. Francis Xavier. Why are you back?"

"Oh."

Tenny looked away. But in the split second before he did, Bethesda thought she detected a look of distress glinting in her friend's eyes, a look suggestive of some deep and mysterious truth buried like pirate's treasure. Then he shrugged, climbed onto his bike, and pointed it down Chesterton Street.

"It's a long story," he said. "I'll tell you another time."

"Oh. Okay. Well, see you soon."

He was already in motion. Bethesda waited as her co-detective pedaled unevenly away, then retreated into the house. Her father was shuffling around in the kitchen, opening and shutting cupboards. "Tabasco . . . Tabasco . . . where art thou, Tabasco?"

Bethesda told herself it was no big deal, that Tenny was entitled to his privacy. But his weird silence ("It *was* weird, right?" she asked herself, replaying the moment and categorizing it definitively as weird) stung a little. Master Detective Bethesda Fielding returned to the kitchen and served herself a bowl of chili and a big hunk of cornbread, feeling increasingly like she had two mysteries on her hands, instead of one.

22

Can Your Hemispheric Placebo Bear Fruit?

While Bethesda Fielding and Tenny Boyer were working their way through their list of suspects, Marisol Pierce was in her bedroom, the windows thrown open to let in the cool autumn breeze, painting trees. She had unrolled a long piece of butcher paper from the roll she'd bought at the art supply store, and taped it up so it covered one whole wall of the room. Slowly but surely, her brush dipping deftly in and out of golds and greens and browns, she filled the paper with a long, lovely line of pines and firs.

Outside her door her little cousins, visiting from Puerto Rico, cavorted noisily in the hall, shooting each other with water pistols. "Got you!" "No you didn't!" "You're all wet!" "No I'm not!"

It was rude not to be playing with them, but Marisol tuned out the noise and focused on her trees, carefully adding a cluster of russet leaves to a copse of young oaks. Marisol was, as her grandmother always said, "rather a solitary soul." In the two years since they'd moved to this area, she still hadn't become terribly close with many kids at Mary Todd Lincoln; frankly, she had no idea why Chester Hu had invited her to be part of this video project. But he had, and she was secretly delighted. Marisol was happy for any excuse to do some painting. She loved making art, loved the intense focus it required.

The tricky part was the people. Chester and the others had decided that the backdrops for the video should be filled with people: People playing, people climbing ropes, people looking through binoculars and building fires.

"Of course," Marisol had said, not wanting to disappoint the group. "I can do that."

But the truth was, when she drew people, they had these stubby little limbs and faces, like sea turtles standing on their hind legs. Marisol sighed and stepped back from her work in progress as her grandmother cracked open her door. "Excuse me, Madame Artiste? I am taking your cousins for ice cream. Are you coming?"

"No, thanks. I really need to finish this."

"Well, it's incredible so far, my darling. I love the little sea turtles."

When her grandmother closed the door, Marisol put down her brush and picked up her phone. There was another girl in the eighth grade whose artwork she had admired, but Marisol barely knew her. The idea of calling a person she barely knew, out of the blue, made Marisol so nervous that the roof of her mouth got all dry, like it was coated with the dust from the bottom of a jar of peanuts.

But this was important. This was Taproot Valley.

Lisa Deckter was out walking her dog when her phone started vibrating her in pocket.

She froze. Henry tugged at the leash.

The phone vibrated again.

It's her, thought Lisa, feeling the chill of a cool autumn breeze as it snuck under the collar of her jean jacket. *It's Pamela. She knows.*

The phone vibrated. Lisa remained still. *I should just answer it. Just get this over with. Admit the whole thing.*

Henry barked, straining toward an inviting pile of red and orange leaves at the other end of the park. The phone vibrated again, and finally Lisa dipped her hand into her pocket, took a deep breath, and looked at the display.

Oh. Phew.

It was a number she didn't recognize. She flipped the phone open, allowed Henry to lead her to the leaves. "Oh, hey, it's Marisol Pierce," said the voice on the other end. "Um, can I ask you—are you good at drawing people?"

A few weeks earlier, Braxton Lashey had been simultaneously doing the dishes and buying movie tickets over the phone when the cell phone slipped out from under his ear and fell in the garbage disposal.

He fished it out, but now some of the buttons didn't work anymore, and the autofill function was kind of out of control. So when Braxton texted his buddy Ellis Walters, at about four thirty on Saturday afternoon— right as Marisol Pierce was hanging up with Lisa Deckter—to say CAN YOU HELP ME FIND A PLACE TO RENT A BEAR SUIT, Ellis got a text that said CAN YOUR HEMISPHERIC PLACEBO BEAR FRUIT?

Ellis texted back THAT MAKES NO SENSE.

Braxton started to type a reply, then opted to just call. "Yo. Chester's making this video to save Taproot Valley, and I need to dress in a bear suit and fall down a flight of stairs."

"Oh," said Ellis. "That still makes no sense."

Nevertheless, half an hour later, in a costume shop owned by a friend of Ellis's mom from church, the two boys were intently debating which kind of bear would be funniest.

"I'm thinking grizzly," said Braxton.

"No, man, panda," countered Ellis. "You gotta go panda."

It was the same all over town. Everyone on the Save Taproot Valley team, everyone Chester had gathered at the picnic benches on Wednesday afternoon, was way too psyched to keep it to themselves.

"Hey, Tucker, you've got a digital video camera, right?" said Todd.

"Ezra? It's Rory. What rhymes with fire ants?"

"Shelly! Can you come to my room for a second?" yelled Suzie. "I have a question about site hosting."

"Um, Reenie? It's Natasha. I need someone really smart to help me figure out these dances. You're, like, a genius, right?"

Only one person, of all the many people invited that day to help out, declined the invitation.

"Victor? Hey! It's Carmine. Dude, so, Lindsey heard from Lisa, who got a call from Marisol Pierce, about this crazy video project that Chester is organizing. The Save Taproot Valley project? Have you heard about this?"

"Yes. I have," Victor replied coolly. He was in his room, working on the flood plain he and Bethesda were building for Mr. Darlington's class, carefully placing doomed LEGO people in their rickety wooden seaside huts.

"Well, so, we're all gonna meet after school this week to make the movie. Are you in?"

"No. I'm busy."

"But I didn't even tell you what day yet."

Victor Glebe hung up the phone and got back to work on his diorama.

23

Week of a Thousand Quizzes

Cruising down Hallway C on Monday morning, Ida Finkleman hummed brightly to herself from the overture to the 1786 opera *The Marriage of Figaro*, her hands conducting an invisible orchestra. For all her newfound love of rock and roll, Mozart would always be her heart's darling, and the *Figaro* overture her favorite melody to hum when she found herself in a cheery mood.

It was a new week, and Ms. Finkleman had a feeling that everything at Mary Todd Lincoln was returning, ever so slowly, to normal. She looked forward to a nice, calm week, during which she would focus entirely on her educational responsibilities, with no special projects or awkward student conversations to distract her. She pushed open the door of the Band and Chorus room, singing a snatch of *Figaro*'s delightful opening duet, expecting to find her classroom as she had left it on Friday afternoon: blinds drawn, instruments in their cases, three rows of music stands arranged on the risers.

What she saw instead was this: Todd Spolin in the back of the room, making a heavy metal face and straddling an electric guitar like a witch on a broomstick; Natasha Belinsky guiding Marisol Pierce and Pamela Preston through some sort of complicated three-step dance; Kevin McKelvey at the piano and Rory Daas *on* the piano, scribbling in a notebook; and Chester Hu circulating among them all with a clipboard, making notes and grinning. Oh, and there was Braxton Lashey, standing on the top riser, balancing precariously on one foot, wearing the body, but not the head, of a bear costume.

A nice, calm week, Ms. Finkleman thought, shaking her head. *Everything back to normal. Right.*

"Excuse me?" she said, cupping her hands together and speaking loudly over Kevin's piano playing. "Anyone?"

Kevin stopped and pushed back the bench. "Oh, hi. Good morning. Hello. We're using your room to work on this sort of project-type thing." Ms. Finkleman crossed her arms and cocked an eyebrow, and Kevin hastily added, "It was Chester's idea."

Chester Hu approached sheepishly. "We're just working out a few details. Hope you don't mind."

Don't ask, said the little voice in Ms. Finkleman's head as the other kids filed out, Braxton lugging his bear head awkwardly under one arm. *For the love of mike, don't ask.*

But she couldn't help herself. "The details of *what*, Chester?"

Speaking quickly, bouncing on his toes, Chester explained the whole project to Ms. Finkleman—the song, the video, the website, the fund-raising campaign. As he spoke, Ms. Finkleman smiled more and more, deeply impressed by the enterprising spirit and creativity on display. "And this was your idea, Chester?"

"Oh, you know," said Chester, shrugging and looking away, embarrassed. "Kind of a group effort."

Chester left—but any hope Ms. Finkleman might have had that the rest of her day would be relatively normal was dispelled a few minutes later.

"Good morning, people of Mary Todd Lincoln."

The P.A. crackled to life just as the school day began, when Ms. Finkleman's first-period sixth graders were still filing in, finding their seats, tossing down their backpacks, and scarfing their last bites of Pop-Tart.

"This is your principal. So listen up."

✦ ✦ ✦

As she listened to the hard, cold voice of Principal Van Vreeland over the P.A., Bethesda Fielding gritted her teeth and looked at the ceiling.

"It has been two weeks since our trophy was stolen, and the responsible party has yet to come forward. Apparently a further inducement is required."

Already, the other kids in Ms. Fischler's class were glancing over at Bethesda, ready to hold her accountable for whatever new punishment their principal had dreamed up.

"I will be instructing every teacher in this school, in every subject, to begin writing questions. Because two weeks from today, all students will be having a test or a quiz, in every subject, every day, for one whole week."

Bethesda groaned.

The students around her groaned.

Ms. Fischler, frozen at the front of the room with chalk in hand, also groaned.

"Unless, that is," the principal continued, "the trophy is returned first." The groaning grew in volume and intensity. "Now. Some of you will have noticed that this Week of a Thousand Quizzes will be taking place the third week in October, the same week our eighth-grade friends would have been on their outdoor education trip. That week, of course, is wide open at present."

Bethesda closed her eyes, but she could still feel the stares—a classroom full of angry math students, craning their necks, pivoting their chairs to glare at her, everyone thinking the same thing:

All your fault . . . this is all your fault!

Meanwhile, in the Band and Chorus room, Ms. Finkleman did some quiet, restrained groaning of her own. *A week's worth of quiz questions? For music students? Plus,* her fellow teachers would be hounding her to give it another shot, to return to the Main Office to beg Principal Van Vreeland for mercy all over again.

She sighed and tapped her baton for quiet. *A nice, normal week . . .*

Chester, in his seat in Dr. Capshaw's room, exhaled and shook his head. Principal Vreeland had it backward. There was no way whoever stole that stupid trophy would come forward now.

This video better work, he thought. *Man oh man, it better work.*

24

Set You Free

Suspect #1: Kevin McKelvey

"Skabimple," murmured Bethesda as she cracked open the door and peeked into the Band and Chorus room. It was lunchtime that Monday, time for her first official interrogation, and here was her first suspect. Kevin McKelvey, the Piano Kid, sat at the beat-up Steinway in his blue blazer and dress pants, as Bethesda had seen him so many times before. Until last year, Kevin McKelvey played only classical music, as he had his entire piano-playing career, which began when he was two and a half years old. But then came the Choral Corral, and the Rock Show, and now Kevin played *everything*, from pop-punk to boogie-woogie to bebop.

But what on earth was he playing now?

"Once upon a time . . . there were some kids who had a dream!" Kevin sang in a high, warbling voice, his fingers gently caressing the keys. "A dream sweet and delicious . . . as a bowl of peach ice cream."

Bethesda couldn't bring herself to interrupt. Maintaining the soft vamp with one hand, Kevin reached up with the other and flipped a page of the blue spiral notebook balanced on the top of the piano.

"The dream we had was so unique . . . to sleep in bunks, climb some trees, and not shower"—Kevin's voice jumped into a comical falsetto—"for a weeeeeeeek!"

Bethesda yelped with laughter. Kevin jumped in his seat and turned around.

"Sorry, sorry . . . ," Bethesda said between giggles. "That is *awesome*."

"It's getting there, uh, you know. It's getting there." Kevin held up the spiral notebook. "Rory wrote the lyrics. My job is just to, er, to make it sing. Make it sound pretty."

Bethesda exhaled the last of her laughter, stepped inside, and settled down in Ms. Finkleman's chair. Principal Van Vreeland's announcement that morning, galling as it was, had only reinforced her determination. She and Tenny were going to work their way through the suspects and find this thief. No doubt about it.

"So, Kevin," Bethesda said, keeping her voice nice and light. "You still play in here a lot after school, right?"

"Uh, yeah. Sure. I'd say about, maybe, half the time. When I play rock at home, my father refuses to come out of his room, and my mother makes all these faces." He demonstrated, screwing up his mouth like he was sucking on a lemon. "So I end up practicing in here a lot. Sometimes Ms. Finkleman is here, grading papers or whatever, and sometimes I'm alone."

"And you use the key Mr. Ferrars gave you?"

Kevin looked up, alarmed. His fingers hovered uncertainly above the piano. "Um . . . well . . ."

"It's okay," she said, reassuringly. "You promised you wouldn't mention it. Forget I asked."

Bethesda tipped him a wink, plucked a sharpened #2 pencil from her pocket, and opened the Semi-Official Crime-Solving Notebook in her lap. "Now, then," she began. "Two Mondays ago, on the afternoon of the twentieth. Were you here after school on *that* day?"

"What?"

Kevin's entire body grew completely still. He met her searching gaze with eyes wide, his mouth hanging slightly open. She searched his face for a glimmer of guilt, for a telltale flicker of anxiety in his eyes.

But Kevin didn't look guilty. He just looked hurt. "You, um . . . you think I stole the trophy?"

Bethesda flushed and reached up to fuss with her glasses.

"Well . . . I mean . . ."

"You do! You think I stole the trophy!"

"I didn't say that. You're, um, you're one of a number of possible suspects, that's all."

"A number of possible suspects," Kevin echoed, his wounded expression now hardening into something more like anger. He snapped shut the wooden housing of the keyboard, leaned back stiffly, and crossed his arms over his chest, the sleeves of his blue blazer bunching up at the elbows.

"It's just . . . you know," Bethesda stammered feebly. "*Somebody* stole it."

"Undoubtedly," Kevin said. "But, also, a lot of people *didn't* steal it. Why aren't I on that list?"

The truth was, Bethesda and Tenny had no motive for Kevin, and he definitely didn't *sound* guilty. On the other hand, if he was guilty, that's exactly how he would want to sound! Bethesda rubbed her eyes under her glasses with her index fingers and tried to concentrate.

"Let's take a step back. I just need you to tell me if you saw or heard anything unusual around here after school that day."

"All right. Hold on." Shaking his head with annoyance, Kevin hunched over on the bench and dug around in the red-and-black messenger bag, stenciled with the logo of the Sydney Municipal Orchestra, that he lugged around instead of a backpack.

"Where is it?" he asked himself quietly.

Bethesda felt the same rushing sensation in her bloodstream that she had just before Mr. Ferrars told her about the keys. Her foot danced on the crisp mauve rug beneath Ms. Finkleman's desk. There was a clue in that fancy bag of his. She could just feel it.

"Here we go," Kevin announced, when at last he resurfaced clutching a small, thin black notebook, its white pages filled with Kevin's careful handwriting. "My practice diary. I, uh, I know it sounds—whatever—but I write down exactly what I work on every day, and for exactly how long." As Kevin riffled through the little book, Bethesda felt a keen flash of envy, not only for Kevin's incredible talent, but for his dedication.

"Oh, right," he said suddenly. "I actually *didn't* practice here two Mondays ago."

Bethesda's heart sank.

"I was going to," Kevin continued. "But someone else was using the room."

"Ms. Finkleman?"

He looked up. "No. A kid. Two kids, actually."

Bingo. Bethesda rolled herself a few inches closer to Kevin on Ms. Finkleman's spinny black desk chair. "Two kids were in here? Kevin, who were they?"

He shrugged. "I don't know."

"What do you mean you don't know?"

"Geez, Bethesda, take it easy. When I heard someone was in here, I turned around and went home. That's called minding your own business."

She ignored the swipe. "You're sure it was *two* kids?"

"I heard two voices. A girl and a boy. And they were singing."

Bethesda's feet rat-a-tatted on the floor like drumsticks. Her gaze jumped from one end of the Band and Chorus room to the other, as if she could force this mysterious pair to materialize from the room's darkened corners. Two kids. A boy and a girl. Singing!

"So, what were they singing?"

"Oh, it was sort of a goofy thing. Let's see . . ." Kevin tilted his head toward the ceiling, summoning back the song, and Bethesda watched his hands. His fingers were thinking, too, arranging themselves in little clusters on the keys, trying and rejecting possibilities, conjuring a melody remembered from a couple weeks ago. "The boy was doing most of the singing, as I recall, with the girl just kind of chiming in." Kevin tried out a chord, paused, shifted his fingers, tried another. "There we go."

He began to sing.

"Locked up too long! You been locked up too long! And that's wrong, so wrong!"

As always, all the hesitancy of Kevin McKelvey's speaking voice disappeared when he sang, and he belted the silly little lyrics clear and strong. Kevin's fingers bounced through the simple, three-chord pattern. "Turn to me! Turn to me!" he sang. "And I'll set you free!"

His voice popped up an octave for the big finish. "Oh you sweet thing . . . I'm gonna set . . . yooooooooou . . . freeeeee!"

Then, just like that, Kevin stopped singing and shrugged. "Then I left." Bethesda refrained from pointing out to Kevin that, for someone minding his own business, he had heard an awful lot of the song.

"So, detective?" he asked. "Am I free to go?"

After Kevin left, Bethesda took his place at the piano

bench. She plunked at random keys, singing lightly to herself, wondering what it all could mean.

"Turn to me . . . and I'll set you free . . ."

Suspect #2: Guy Ficker

Whoosh!

In one easy, graceful movement, Guy Ficker crouched, sprang, took to the air, pumped his legs, and sent the basketball *swooshing* noiselessly into the net. He snagged his own rebound, twirled on his heels, and bounced the ball over to Tenny Boyer.

"Ow," said Tenny, flinching, as it sprang up from the blacktop and stung his palms.

"Shake it off, man," said Guy. "Your shot."

Tenny shaded his eyes with one hand and dribbled awkwardly with the other. They were at the Remsen Playground after school, playing a game called Horse, where the goal is for each player to match the shot the other guy just took. If you missed the shot, you got a letter. The first person with all five letters lost. They'd been playing for six minutes. Tenny had HORS, and Guy had nothing.

"Hey, um, Guy. Can I ask you a quick question, dude?"

Guy scowled. "Take your shot, Tenny."

Maybe this was a bad idea. Tenny had figured it would be smart to do his first suspect interrogation here, in an atmosphere where Guy was most comfortable—on the court, out in the open air. Nearby, a couple elementary school kids were whacking a tennis ball back and forth; toddlers tottered around in the sandbox; an older kid in a baseball cap was sitting on the playground equipment, humming to himself. It was the perfect setting, Tenny thought, to interrogate a sports person like Guy. People are most relaxed when they're doing something they love, something they're good at. Tenny had a recent painful memory of his mom coming to talk about something Very Serious and Important, and how agitated and annoying the whole conversation had been—mainly because she insisted he sit with her at the kitchen table. All he wanted the whole time was to be in the basement, with his guitar, so he could strum chords or lightly fingerpick while she was talking.

"C'mon, Tenny. *Shoot.*"

Tenny jumped and spun around, as Guy had just done so effortlessly, and hurled the ball in the general direction of the net. It flew past the backboard toward the metal fence separating the court from the slides and swings. The older kid in the baseball cap at the top of the slide stopped humming and barked in surprise as the ball rattled against the fence.

Tenny was *not* a sports person. "That's E for me," he said, relieved. "You win."

"Play again?"

"Uh . . ." Not waiting for an answer, Guy scooped up the ball, dribbled twice, and drove in one easy motion down the court for a smooth, gliding layup. "Your shot, man."

Okay, this was *definitely* a bad idea. Tenny was starting to feel like he'd been out here forever, pretending to like basketball. He dribbled twice (as Guy had done), drove in toward the basket in one easy motion (as Guy had done), and then heaved the ball as high and hard as he could, way over the fence. It landed with a distant thump, somewhere on the far side of the swing set.

"Oops," said Tenny.

"Wow," said Guy. With no rebound to grab, his hands flapped helplessly against his hips.

"Oh, hey," said Tenny. "So here's what I wanted to ask you . . ."

They sat with their backs against the fence, and soon Tenny got all the info he was after. He confirmed, first of all, that Guy had been angry (was *still* pretty angry, in fact) about not being able to use the gym to practice for his archery tournament. "Double V says I can use it every day for a week," he complained, using a nickname for Principal Van Vreeland popular among the cool kids, "and then I get the boot so Pamela and the gymnastics people can have it. Lame, right?"

"Totally."

Motive confirmed! Tenny thought. *Sweetness.*

But, as it turned out, Guy had an alibi, too. "Monday? Five forty-five? Sure, man. I was at the mall. Went with my dad to look at baseball mitts, then to dinner. You can ask Tasharoo about the dinner part."

"Um . . . Tasharoo?"

"Natasha, man. We're kind of, like, family friends. My folks have known hers since we were kids. We go to dinner every once in a while at that seafood place, Pirate Sam's. Family tradition, you know?"

Tenny did know. Pirate Sam's was a family tradition kind of place. There was a period, years ago, when his own family went every Sunday night for dinner. He always got the Golden Fish Nuggets, which came in a cardboard chest.

"That answer all your questions, Tenners?" said Guy, hauling himself up from the patch of asphalt where they'd settled themselves. Tenny smiled bashfully, surprised at how proud he was that Guy had graced him with a nickname.

He was still smiling when he heard a voice from the playground side, yelling, "Heads up!" The basketball was on its way back, and Tenny just had time to realize that it was Todd Spolin who had thrown it, and that it was *Todd* who'd been sitting there on the playground equipment, the whole time they were talking—before the ball sailed over the fence in a wide arc and bonked him in the nose.

"Ooh! Tenners!" said Guy, wincing sympathetically.

"Not a sports person," Tenny mumbled as spots danced before his eyes.

25

The Person in the Upstairs Bathroom

Late that night, in a house across town, in an innocuous upstairs bathroom decorated with olive-green towels and lavender-scented soap, a pair of eyes stared back from a mirror.

It was a typical bathroom mirror with a simple brass frame, hung between a pair of charming seaside watercolors. As for the eyes, they were clouded and dark as they narrowed beneath a troubled brow.

These were the eyes of a person crafting a scheme—a scheme to thwart Bethesda Fielding's ongoing investigation. Unbeknownst to Bethesda, someone had been watching her as she developed her leads, as she teamed up with Tenny, as they made their plans and sought out their suspects. Someone had been hiding behind poles, ducking unnoticed through crowded hallways, paying careful attention to her every move.

Bethesda was clever. A little too clever. She was determined to solve the mystery, and for the person in the upstairs bathroom, that was a problem.

Something had to be done. Bethesda Fielding had to be stopped.

A rap came at the door, and the person in the upstairs bathroom jumped in surprise.

"God! What?"

"You almost done in there? I really gotta pee, sweets."

Man! Couldn't a person get five minutes in this house to hatch a nefarious plot?

26

We're Going to Need More Snacks

As soon as school ended on Wednesday, Chester met up with the rest of his team to bike to Tamarkin Reservoir, the big grassy field where they'd be shooting the main scenes of the video. They were all going over as a group: Chester, Rory, Marisol, Kevin, Braxton, Suzie, Todd, and Natasha, the whole team except Pamela, who insisted on walking. "If I'm late, you can shoot some other part first," she said. "I am *not* mushing up my hair in a bike helmet before being filmed."

Chester coasted at the front of the pack of cyclists, weaving back and forth, feeling the gentle breeze on his legs. "Oh, hey," Rory said suddenly as they turned off Friedman to head toward the reservoir. "I keep meaning to tell you. I asked a couple people to help out. That cool?"

It took Chester a second to realize that Rory was

talking to him—he kept forgetting that he was in charge. "Sure," he said. "Of course."

"Yeah, actually, I invited a couple people, too," said Natasha.

"Me, too," Marisol added quietly.

Chester shrugged. "That's cool."

What Chester didn't yet know was that the couple people Rory had called had each called a couple people, and each of those people had called a couple of their own. The same was true for Natasha's couple people, and Marisol's, and Braxton's . . . and though Ms. Fischler wasn't on hand to explain how the total number of people had grown through exponential multiplication, the result was clear when they crested the final hill and kickstanded their bikes at the edge of Tamarkin Reservoir. In the low, green gully, dozens and dozens and dozens of kids were milling around. It was practically the entire eighth grade, along with tons of sixth and seventh graders, plus kids Chester didn't even recognize, kids from other schools or something. Scanning the crowd, amazed, Chester spotted Kelly Deal and Peter Holsapple, both of whom had graduated last year and were at Pilverton High now.

And then, as Chester and his posse got off their bikes, the whole huge crowd burst into applause.

"Let's do it!" shouted Ellis Walters, yelling through cupped hands from the back of the crowd. "Let's save Taproot Valley!"

Chester couldn't help but notice the one person who was *not* a part of this giant crowd—his best friend, Victor Glebe. Well, no time to worry about it now. Chester turned his mind to making fresh plans: Natasha would need to build more people into her choreography; Kevin could add more harmony parts to the song. . . .

Chester turned to Todd Spolin, who happened to be standing beside him, and said, "We're going to need more snacks."

What Ida Finkleman should have been doing, at that moment, was writing quiz questions. Like every teacher in school, she had two weeks to prepare an entire week's worth of questions, a massively time-consuming proposition. But here she was instead, watching thoughtfully through the chain-link fence that separated Patterson Lane from Tamarkin Reservoir. She watched as the kids unrolled the long, beautiful murals that Marisol and Lisa had painted and strung them carefully from the trees. She watched Braxton put on his grizzly bear costume, backward, then watched him take it off and put it on again correctly. She watched Tenny coach Todd on how to place his fingers on the guitar, to pretend to play the solo he'd recorded. She watched Chester set up the shots and cry "Action!" When the Save Taproot Valley song came blaring out of Shelly's laptop, Ms. Finkleman noted the compositional virtuosity that Kevin had brought to the project and chuckled at Rory's strained but charming rhyme of the words "bonfire" and "quagmire."

Surely this video would be, if not brilliant, at least utterly unique. But whether it would raise enough money to send the kids on their outdoor education trip was a very different question. Four thousand, seven hundred and thirty-six dollars was a *lot* of money, and the scheduled departure date was less than two weeks away.

Ms. Finkleman turned from the fence and walked back down Patterson Lane, toward the school, to get her car and drive home.

If only there was something she could do to help.

While all the other kids were at Tamarkin Reservoir, no doubt having the time of their lives, Bethesda Fielding biked home alone. No one besides Tenny had even told her about the Save Taproot Valley project, let alone invited her, and she was trying very hard not to be bummed about it. Bethesda loved fund-raising projects! When she was nine, she'd made almost a hundred dollars in four hours of selling lemonade, by having kids pay an extra dollar to squeeze the lemons themselves, using a shiny silver handheld juicer. Less work, more money!

Bethesda chastised herself sternly: Does Sherlock Holmes get jealous? What about Charlie Chan? Does Wellington Wolf, Jungle P.I., get all mopey because he can't play with the other animals! Of course not! Why do you think they call them *lone* wolves?

Chortling at her own joke, Bethesda didn't notice until the last second a garbage can that had tipped over and rolled out onto the sidewalk. She jerked the handlebars of her blue Schwinn, lurched hard, and almost hit another cyclist who was passing her on the right.

"Hey! Watch it!" said the other girl, glaring backward over her shoulder.

It was Reenie Maslow. Of course.

"Shoot. Sorry, Reenie."

Bethesda pumped her legs a few times, giving herself a burst of speed to catch up. Her self–pep talk notwithstanding, Bethesda was psyched to have someone else to talk to. "So," she said, pulling up to keep pace with Reenie, "you weren't invited to do this video thing either, huh?"

"Of course I was. Everyone was. I just didn't have time."

Well, gee, Bethesda thought. *Thanks for making me feel better.*

They biked in silence for a couple minutes, Bethesda struggling the whole time to think of something else to say, Reenie just staring straight ahead, the sun gleaming off her silver helmet. When Bethesda turned off Friedman Street onto Dunwiddie, Reenie did too. *Whoa*, thought Bethesda. *Two short, book-loving, glasses-wearing girls with reddish-tannish hair who live in the same neighborhood!* And yet . . .

"So, what, are you, like, following me?" Reenie asked abruptly, shooting Bethesda an annoyed look.

"No! Reenie, I . . . I . . ."

Reenie stood up on her pedals, knapsack balanced high on her back like a soldier's duffel, cranked her legs, and zoomed away. Bethesda rolled to a stop and watched her disappear over the horizon.

At home, Bethesda took a Snapple and a bowlful of graham crackers from the kitchen and went upstairs to do homework. Mr. Galloway was giving extra credit to anyone who memorized the Gettysburg Address. But try as she might, Bethesda couldn't get past the "conceived in liberty" part.

Three little letters kept dancing through her mind: IOM.

27

"My Favorite Things"

To the student body, Principal Van Vreeland's proposed Week of a Thousand Quizzes was a grossly unfair punishment; to most of the teachers, it was a huge and unwelcome task. But to Harry Melville, who taught sixth- and seventh-grade Social Studies, it was a dream come true. Some people were good at dancing, while others drove race cars or wrote poems or performed complicated surgeries. Mr. Melville's gift was for writing difficult test questions, and this was his moment to shine.

Since the principal's announcement, he had spent every evening here in his small, comfortable home, settled in a wingback chair behind his rolltop desk, carefully crafting the most delightfully difficult

Social Studies questions he could. Which states voted to ratify the United States Constitution, and which did not? Who was President Washington's secretary of the treasury? Who was his *deputy* secretary of the treasury? In 250 words, describe General Benedict Arnold's motivation for betraying the Continental Army. Now do it in 500 words.

Stopping to think between questions, Mr. Melville stroked his bushy white beard, singing happily to himself. "Raindrops on something and something on kittens . . . something some something . . ."

"Harry? You have a visitor."

Easing nervously into the room, Ida Finkleman nodded a polite thank-you to Sally Ann Melville while the hardest teacher in school waved her into a chair.

"Why, Ms. Finkleman!" Mr. Melville bellowed affably. "To what do I owe the pleasure?"

She looked a bit taken aback by his good spirits. "Um, well . . . you've been at the school a long time, and I thought you could help me. You see, I'd like to help out some students of mine."

Mr. Melville's famous eyebrows, white and thick as an arctic forest, arranged themselves into two skeptical arches. "Now why," he asked, "would you want to do that?"

But as it turned out, Mr. Melville *did* know a way to help. Exactly as Ms. Finkleman had suspected, the gruff old social studies teacher, at some point in his many years of teaching, had heard of a certain program. "Well, not really a program," said Mr. Melville, digging an old, yellowed pamphlet from a drawer of the rolltop desk. "It's just this man from St. Louis. A man with a *lot* of money."

Mr. Melville cautioned her that the Piccolini-Provokovsky grant had no formal application process, and that he had never heard of anyone actually winning it. In other words, he said, the whole thing was silly. "But as a wise man once said," he concluded, referring to himself, "your days on this earth belong to you, and are yours to waste."

And so, at 10:30 p.m., Ms. Finkleman was in her brown bathrobe, in her cozy recliner with her computer open on her lap, sipping a cup of Sleepytime tea and composing an email to a very rich man from St. Louis named Ivan Piccolini-Provokovsky. She labored over this email, writing and rewriting, trying to get it perfect.

Dear Mr. Piccolini-Provokovsky,

went the email so far.

> My name is Ida Finkleman, and I serve as
> Band and Chorus instructor at Mary Todd
> Lincoln Middle School. Certain of my students
> are engaged in a project that I feel you will find
> most intriguing. It involves

Involves? For heaven's sake, Ida. She tapped Delete a bunch of times, and wrote the sentence again.

> It showcases an impressive display of talent,
> an impassioned plea, and a mighty animal of the
> forest tumbling down a flight of stairs.

That seemed about right.

The rest of the email gave a precise and detailed description of the "Save Taproot Valley" video project; a bit of background on Chester and his academic career thus far; and, of course, the most important part of all. The request.

Satisfied at last, Ms. Finkleman crossed her fingers and hit Send.

28

Possibilities

Suspect #3: Janitor Steve

"Excuse me? Hey, sorry . . ." Tenny cracked open the door and peered into the janitor's closet in the basement. "Um . . ."

"Eh? Who's that?"

Janitor Steve, in black work pants and a thick denim shirt, was seated on an upside-down mop bucket, combing out the bristles of a double-wide broom. "Just keeping the old broom clean," he said, gesturing for Tenny to enter. "Clean broom, clean floor. Clean floor, clean mind. Clean mind . . ." He paused. "Clean pants? I don't know. What do you want, kid?"

"Huh? Oh . . . right. Okay . . ."

Tenny hadn't thought about how to start this interrogation. He was just glad to be down here, and not to be spending another lunch period fielding the same annoying questions over and over, from Tucker and Ezra and all the rest of 'em.

"So, what're you doing back, man?"

"Oh, you know, long story . . ."

Tenny was so sick of the conversations, and the whispers, and the rumors . . . oh, man, the stupid rumors. He'd been expelled for fighting. He'd been expelled for stealing. He'd given everyone at St. Francis Xavier—kids, teachers, maintenance staff, everyone—the chicken pox . . . on purpose.

"This might sound kind of weird," he said to Janitor Steve. "It's about the trophy."

"Oh?" Janitor Steve stopped cleaning and cocked an eyebrow.

"Yeah. Do you know something about it?"

"I sure do," said Janitor Steve, heaving himself up from the bucket and carefully hanging his broom back on the wall.

"You do?"

"Yup." He turned and looked right at Tenny. "I know who stole it, and why."

Suspect #4: Lisa Deckter

As Janitor Steve told Tenny Boyer what he had to say,

Bethesda was cornering her own next suspect at the top of Stairwell #1. She extended her arm to the banister, blocking Lisa Deckter from going down. It was just the two of them in the empty stairwell; everyone else had already gotten their lunches and gone outside.

"Hey," said Bethesda. "We need to talk."

"Okay," Lisa replied warily, tearing the wrapper off a gluten-free health and energy bar. Bethesda, in her mind, pulled down the brim of her battered detective's fedora, readying herself for a daring gambit. Lisa had no alibi that Bethesda knew of, plus a compelling motive, having placed second behind Pamela in the gymnastics tournament. It was time for a classic tactic from the private investigator's tool kit: the big bluff.

"I know, Lisa," Bethesda said coolly. "I know what you did."

Lisa's mouth dropped open, and she lowered the health bar slowly from her lips.

"H-how. . . ," she stammered. "How did you know?"

Whoa, Bethesda thought, startled. *That worked* great.

"Wait. What?"

"I'm telling you, kid." Janitor Steve deepened his

voice, like a camp counselor at a bonfire. "The person who stole that trophy wasn't a person at all."

"So—you mean—it was . . ." Tenny scratched his head, confused. "A robot?"

"No."

"A shark?"

"No!"

"Um . . ."

"Why don't I just tell you. It was the vengeful spirit of Little Ronnie Farnsworth."

"Wait. *What?*"

Janitor Steve nodded gravely. "Ronnie Farnsworth was a boy who went here when I did. Everybody picked on him a lot, because he talked to himself and smelled kind of weird. Ronnie always swore he'd have his revenge."

"Whoa."

"Yeah. And now, starting at the beginning of the semester, I've been hearing him, banging on things, making all sortsa eerie noises in the pipes. Also, I think he moved my ladder."

Tenny didn't really believe in ghosts, but Janitor Steve was giving him the heebie-jeebies. "So, this Ronnie guy. When did he die?"

"Die? Oh no, he's fine. He drives a bus, over in

Bellville. He's actually in my book club. It's his *spirit*, kid. It's his vengeful spirit that haunts us. Or, *haunted* us. I actually haven't heard a peep from that old ghost since he got the trophy. Not a peep."

"Huh. Well, uh—thanks, man. Thanks a lot."

"Sure thing. Hey, leave the door open a crack, will ya? Fumes."

"I mean, of course I wanted that gymnastics trophy. I wanted it bad."

Bethesda held her breath and leaned against the stair rail, tense with anticipation as Lisa's confession unspooled. "It's so big and beautiful. Plus, you know what the runner-up got? A gift certificate to Pirate Sam's." She looked ruefully at her gluten-free, nut-free, egg-free soy bar. "I can eat literally nothing there."

"And thus you made your fateful decision," Bethesda proclaimed, thrusting one finger into the air. "You had to have the trophy for your own!"

"Wait. You think *I* stole it?"

Not only did Lisa use the same words Kevin McKelvey had, she stared at Bethesda with the same expression— an open-mouthed mixture of confusion, shock, and pain.

"Of course I didn't steal it! Why would I steal

something I let Pamela win in the first place?"

"What?" Now it was Bethesda's turn to be confused. "What do you mean, you let her win?"

"That's what I was just telling you. It's so important to Pamela to be the best at everything. So I purposely messed up my back handspring, so she could win the trophy.

"Oh. Well, that's . . ." Bethesda smiled weakly. "That was really nice."

"Seriously, Bethesda? You think *I* stole it?"

"No. No . . . I just." *Don't say it, Bethesda. Don't say it.* "You know. You're one of a number of possible suspects."

Lisa made a disgusted, huffing noise, said, *"Excuse me,"* and pushed past Bethesda. "Good luck with your mystery," Lisa called back over her shoulder, the cold words echoing in the stairwell.

School ended at three p.m., and Bethesda had arranged to meet with Tenny by the picnic tables at precisely 3:02 to carefully review everything they'd learned so far. By 3:07, she was glancing nervously at the door, bracing herself for the possibility that he wouldn't show, or— considering how weird he was being lately—that he *would* show, but act so distant and unhelpful that she'd wish he hadn't. But at 3:09 Tenny shuffled out, gave a warm little wave, and sat down.

"All right," said Bethesda, laying out her index cards in a neat square in front of her. "Tell me everything."

"Okay . . . let's see . . ."

Carefully, point by point, they went over their interrogations of the last three days. Tenny described his game of Horse with Guy Ficker, skipping over his sorry lack of basketball skills. He explained about Guy's monthly dinner with Natasha's family at Pirate Sam's, and said how Todd Spolin had appeared on the playground, somewhat oddly, out of nowhere. Bethesda said "hmm," but reminded him that Todd wasn't even on their suspect list—he never had a key.

They laughed about Janitor Steve and the vengeful spirit of Little Ronnie Farnsworth, until something occurred to Bethesda. What if the custodian was making the whole thing up? Maybe to deflect suspicion, because he was the one who did it?

"Totally possible," said Tenny. "I gotta tell you, that guy is a whole mystery just himself."

Then Bethesda told Tenny about Lisa Deckter's confession, about her interview with Kevin and what the Piano Kid had overheard—the mysterious pair in the chorus room, singing their strange, silly, catchy song.

"Yeah," Tenny said. "But how do you know Kevin is telling the truth?"

"What, you think he made it up? Could he even do that?"

"Dude," said Tenny, shrugging. "Of *course* he could! He's Kevin McKelvey. He could make up a whole opera if he wanted to."

And that was that. It was 3:47, and they'd gone over everything there was to go over. Tenny snapped a twig off the big oak tree and fiddled it around in his palms. Bethesda took a deep sip of her Lime-Orange Snapple and slipped a rubber band around their heavily annotated stack of index cards. She snuck a glance at her friend, and her mind jumped to the *other* mystery: Why had Tenny returned from St. Francis Xavier?

Possibility #1: He flunked out.

This seemed a bit farfetched. Sure, Tenny wasn't the greatest student in the world, but could a person really flunk out after only three weeks?

"I should probably jet," Tenny said suddenly, flicking away the broken twig. "I haven't even started this book for Capshaw. What is it? *Animal Crackers?*"

"Farm."

"Farm Crackers? Really?"

Hmm. Maybe it's not that farfetched.

Possibility #2: Tenny was so nostalgic for Mary Todd Lincoln Middle School, he had to come back.

As Tenny and Bethesda rose from the picnic bench, Principal Van Vreeland burst from the building, with Jasper scurrying fretfully at her side. "Is that a smile on your face, young lady?" she demanded, jabbing an angry finger toward Bethesda. "No smiling! No happiness! No one is permitted to be happy until my trophy is returned." As they stormed past on their way to the parking lot, Principal Van Vreeland glared, and Jasper gave Bethesda a furtive, pleading look.

Okay, so Possibility #2 is pretty unlikely, too.

"All right, so, what's the story?" Tenny asked as he dug his iPod out of his bag. "Where are we with this investigation?"

"Unfortunately," Bethesda answered, "we're at the part where I have to interrogate Pamela Preston."

29

Brace Yourself

Suspect #6: Pamela Preston

"I'm at the mall," said Pamela tartly, when Bethesda called her on Saturday morning at 10:45. "By all means, come on by."

So Bethesda Fielding, Master Detective, unchained her blue Schwinn and rode to Pilverton Mall. She walked past the movie theater and the video arcade; she walked past the Arthur Treacher's Fish & Chips and the Sbarro's Pizza in the Food Court, smiling in passing at Chef Pilverton with his big wooden rolling pin; she walked past the Build-a-Bear Workshop and the H&M. She found Pamela Preston just where she said she would be: shopping with Natasha at Brace Yourself, a tiny store on the second floor that sold only bracelets.

Bethesda's theory about Pamela Preston had been simmering in her head for over two weeks now, bubbling away quietly like a pot of her father's chili. There was nothing left to do but confront her and see what happens. *The worse thing she can do is laugh at me,* Bethesda thought. Which, as it turned out, was exactly what happened.

"Oh my god, Pam, that is *so* cute on you!"

"You're right. It is."

Pamela was modeling a pink-and-black bracelet, studying her own arm in the mirror while Natasha oohed and aahed appreciatively. Bethesda muttered *argle bargle* under her breath—she would have preferred to talk to this particular suspect alone. Of course Bethesda had to interrogate Natasha, too, but one thing at a time, right? At least Todd Spolin, who usually traveled with Pamela and Natasha in a little pack, was nowhere to be seen.

"Ah. Detective Fielding," said Pamela, her voice lightly glazed with sarcasm, as she worked the pink-and-black bracelet over her hand and replaced it with something jangly and silver. "How can I help you?"

Pamela smirked, and Natasha shifted uncomfortably, looking like she wished she were somewhere else.

"Well, okay," Bethesda began. "Pam, do you remember when we were on the Hustlin' Pancakes?"

"Of course."

When they were six and seven, and still close friends, Bethesda and Pamela had both been star defensemen on the soccer team sponsored by a popular local diner. "And do you remember the time I twisted my ankle and they had to call off the whole game because I was so hurt? And do you remember how, afterward, my dad took us all out for root beer floats, to make me feel better?"

"I love root beer," Natasha said softly, and smiled awkwardly.

"The truth is—" Bethesda continued, but Pamela cut her off.

"Ooh . . . the truth is, the great Bethesda Fielding faked it! Tsk, tsk." Bethesda winced. Pamela was too smart—she could already see where Bethesda was going. "So, what, you think I stole my own trophy? To get *attention*?"

"Um . . . that's not exactly what I'm saying." In fact, it was. That was *exactly* what she was saying. "I just mean—"

That's when Pamela laughed at Bethesda, tilting her head back to let out a long, pretty laugh, like a tinkle of sleigh bells. "You caught me!" she cried out between giggles. "I did it! Oh, have mercy on me!"

"Pamela."

But she kept right on laughing. Natasha laughed, too, but falteringly, like she didn't really understand what they were laughing about. Bethesda just stood there, looking around the store as the waves of mocking laughter washed over her. This unpleasant interlude was at last interrupted by the high school junior who worked at the store.

"Excuse me? Aren't you that girl who got her trophy stolen?"

Pamela nodded, immediately dropping the laughter and putting back on the tearful, vulnerable expression she'd been wearing for three weeks.

"Oh, wow. I'm so sorry. That bracelet is totally on the house."

"Aw, thank you so much."

Pamela winked brazenly at Bethesda, took Natasha by the arm, and swept out of the store in a cloud of lilac perfume, her new bracelet glittering on her arm. Bethesda sighed, toying idly with the racks of bracelets. Did Pamela really think her theory was as stupid as she acted? Or did she want Bethesda to feel foolish, because she really *did* steal her own trophy?

"Hey. You." The high school girl crossed her arms and scowled. "You gonna buy something or what?"

30

World Premiere

"**N**apkin? Napkin? Has everyone got a napkin?"

Melvin Schwartz, Shelly and Suzie's dad, bustled around the room, trying desperately to keep things as tidy as possible. It was Monday night, and they were all there, the whole original "Save Taproot Valley" crew plus Shelly, all crowded into Mr. Schwartz's home office while Suzie futzed with the big desktop computer. They stood in a loose semicircle, five feet back from the desk, because Mr. Schwartz allowed absolutely, positively *no* snacking near the computer, and there were, naturally, a ton of snacks on hand for the world premiere of "Save Taproot Valley." Not only had Mrs. Schwartz baked snickerdoodles, but Chester, ever mindful of Cousin Ilene's advice, had brought three boxes of Entenmann's apple pies and a dozen Capri Suns.

So the kids stood around talking about the video, about camp, about the five-day nightmare of test-taking they faced in a week—*if* their video didn't do its job. They munched their snacks at the Mr. Schwartz–enforced distance, while Suzie, her face pursed with concentration behind the neon-pink frames of her glasses, made the final tweaks on their masterpiece.

"This is going to be so cool, Chester," said Marisol quietly.

"We'll see," he said, nervous, wiping bits of apple pie off his chin.

Chester just wished Victor Glebe was there to share the moment. But after walking out on the first meeting at the picnic benches, Victor had never returned. He hadn't taken part in the songwriting sessions, nor the days of rehearsal on Saturday and Sunday, not even the video shoot itself.

"All right," said Suzie at last, pushing back from the desk. "Are we ready?"

The video started with a close-up of Pamela. She sang Kevin and Rory's heartfelt opening couplet, about the dream "as sweet and delicious as peach ice cream," and then the second one, about "the cruel and wicked principal / who stole our dreams away, who tore them to pieces and burned them up / like a great big pile of hay."

"Still not crazy about 'great big pile of hay,'" muttered Kevin, and Rory shrugged. Meanwhile, on the screen, the shot widened to reveal a long line of kids, arrayed behind Pamela, singing "ooh" and "aah" and fluttering their fingers like flames. Behind them was the giant woodsy mural, strung between two trees; behind the mural was the lush green field of Tamarkin Reservoir.

"Awesome," said Shelly.

"*So* awesome!" Braxton whooped. Suzie shushed them both.

Then the music really kicked in. First, driving drums (which Chester had contributed himself), then a fierce guitar part, complete with a shot of Todd, standing on a desk in the middle of the field, pretending to play what Tenny had recorded. Then there was a second close-up of Pamela, pouting and contemplating a tree. Then the song jumped into the second section, more driving and rhythmic, with lots of different kids taking turns, singing about what they'd be missing at Taproot Valley:

"Trust falls!"

"Bird calls!"

"Hot dog roastin'!"

"Marshmallow toastin'!"

Ezra popped into the shot upside down, descending from the top of the frame (he was in fact hanging by his knees from a tree branch) to sing Rory's favorite lyric: "And fire ants, crawling in our pants!"

"That is *so* funny, Rory," said Pamela, laughing. This was a significant compliment for a part of the video in which she didn't appear. Rory said, "Thanks," grinned, and ran a hand through his perfect hair.

While the song modulated and dipped in and out of a minor key (Kevin nodding with satisfaction at his compositional cleverness), there was a quick close-up of Pamela. She sang, "Without our trip, we're sad as trolls/ lost in the lonesome valley of our souls!" accompanied by a sweeping shot of the sandbox at Remsen Playground, meant to represent the lonesome valley of their souls. Then there was a shot of a huge group of students down on their knees, begging, their cheeks wet with tears— actually seltzer, daubed on each cheek by Chester with a turkey baster. Then came another close-up of Pamela. Then a bear appeared, for some reason, at the top of a flight of stairs, got angry about something off camera, and fell down the steps.

By the time the video approached its conclusion,

Chester and his team were all clapping and dancing happily around the den, while Mr. Schwartz chased them around with a DustBuster. Natasha, the choreographer, had outdone herself on the last part: a shot of nearly a hundred people in the basin of Tamarkin Reservoir, pretending to ride horses, leaning this way and then that way, all together and then individually, creating a cool rhythmic pattern with their bodies, even as Rory's lyric reached its passionate peak:

"Please, please, please save our trip to outdoor ed! Let us stuff a bunch of nature facts into our heads! Let us go where the salmon swim and the bumblebees play! Make a donation and save the day! And we'll be on our waaaaaaaaaaay!"

The kids in the den sang along with the kids on the screen, holding that big last note even longer than they'd held it in the video, which was for a full ten seconds. When it ended they clapped and hooted like lunatics, hugging and patting each other on the back. Shelly handed out plastic cups and Suzie poured celebratory glasses of sparkling cider. ("Coasters?" said Mr. Schwartz. "Has everyone got a coaster?") Even Natasha and Todd slapped each other an exuberant five, forgetting momentarily that they weren't getting along.

"All right, Suzie," said Chester, when the revelry died down. "Let's post this puppy."

In another part of town, in an upstairs bathroom, someone stared deeply into the bathroom mirror, wondering whether to go through with this crazy stunt.

"I could leave this house right now and go do the worst thing I have ever done. Betray all I've ever believed in, and all I've been taught to believe. Or I can go downstairs, make some hot chocolate, and play Super DonkeyKong on the computer."

For a long moment, the mind behind the face weighed these options—the brow bent with concentration, the eyes troubled and pensive, the mouth watering at the thought of creamy hot chocolate. Then the face disappeared from the mirror, and a moment later a lone, mysterious figure snuck out the bathroom door, tiptoed silently down the stairs, and crept out the front door.

31

The Big-Word Bandit

At the first quack of her Three Ducks Quacking alarm clock, Bethesda Fielding woke up, and she woke up singing.

"Set you free!" she sang as she got dressed. "Set you free!" as she tugged her reddish-tannish hair into barrettes and laced up her Chuck Taylors. "Sweet little thing I'm gonna set you free!"

Yes, the mystery solving was going a bit slower than she had anticipated.

Yes, everyone in school was still mad at her . . . madder than ever, actually, what with the looming Week of a Thousand Quizzes.

And yes, her dad was making chili at 7:45 in the morning, which was kind of gross. But the charity dinner at her mom's law firm was in a couple nights, and her dad, being her dad, still wasn't satisfied with his recipe. She obliged him with a quick taste test, told him it was the best batch yet, and went back to singing.

"You been locked up too long! And that's wrong, so wrong!" Bethesda sang as she hefted her backpack and headed out the front door into the cool mid-October morning. "So turn to me! And I'll set you free!"

She sang in a high, comical falsetto, just as Kevin had. Whoever wrote the song—whether it was a pair of mysterious strangers in the Band and Chorus room, or Kevin improvising it to fool her—it was one heck of a catchy tune.

The song died on Bethesda's lips when she saw her bike.

Her beautiful blue Schwinn with the blue and silver piping was just where she had left it yesterday, chained to the mailbox outside the house, the long, plastic-sheathed handlebars angled toward the road, the chrome gleaming in the sun. But the tires had been deflated, and lay hanging from the scuffed rims, sad, deflated, and saggy.

The thief! Bethesda thought, breaking into a run. *The thief!*

She raced to the road, looked one way and then another, but saw nothing. No stranger booking it down Chesterton Street, no one diving furtively into the bushes. Just a couple of squirrels tussling over a nut on Mrs. Beverly's neatly manicured lawn, looking very much incapable of tampering with a bicycle.

Bethesda returned to her sadly damaged bike and unfolded the note she found Scotch-taped to the handlebars.

BETHESDA! it said.

I MUST ASSERT MOST VOCIFEROUSLY THAT YOU DESIST FROM YOUR INVESTIGATORY EFFORTS WITH ALL DUE HASTE!

"Vociferously?" said Bethesda to the squirrels. "Investigatory?"

Whoever this anonymous bike-vandal was, he or she definitely owned a thesaurus. But the gist of the note was perfectly clear. Somebody out there did not want her to solve this crime. There was no signature. Just the cryptic message, filled with what Ms. Petrides, the seventh-grade English Language Arts teacher, called twenty-five-cent words. And then, on the back in smaller print:

Bethesda stood for a long moment on her lawn. Then she carefully folded up the note, shoved it in her bag, and marched steadily down Chesterton Street, head held high, sneakers crunching on the asphalt. She was a detective on a case, by god, and she had work to do! Truths to ferret out! She was going to solve this mystery, and no cowardly, bike-mangling, thesaurus-hugging maniac was going to get in her way!

Suspect #7: Natasha Belinsky

Bethesda rounded the corner onto Friedman Street and turned into the horseshoe driveway leading to school. And there was her next suspect, sitting at the picnic benches, all alone, as if for a prearranged meeting. *Perfect*, thought Bethesda, striding boldly across the horseshoe driveway.

"Natasha?" she said firmly. "We need to chat."

"Oh." Natasha yawned and smiled weakly. "Okay."

Bethesda, in no mood to beat around the bush, rapidly dispensed with the preliminaries. She told Natasha she knew about the key she'd gotten from Assistant Principal Ferrars, and curtly informed her that she was on the list of potential suspects. Natasha just nodded.

"You went to the mall on the afternoon of Monday, September twentieth, to get your nails done, is that correct?"

"What?" Natasha looked down at her hands, then back up at Bethesda. "Oh. Yeah."

"And then went to dinner with Guy Ficker and his family?"

"Yes. At Pirate Sam's. We had the Arrrgh-Ti-Choke dip." She pronounced the dish like it was written on the menu, with a deep, throaty pirate's argh.

"Arrrgh-Ti-Choke," echoed Bethesda. "Cute."

"What is?"

"Never mind. What time was dinner?"

"Um . . ."

While Bethesda waited for the answer, she glanced at the open notebook in her lap, where she had the timeline carefully penciled in.

"We met at five thirty, I think," said Natasha.

Well, that was that. The bang and the crash were at five forty-five, and the mall was at least a twenty-minute bike ride away. Except then Natasha looked up again, bit her lower lip, and shrugged. "You know, it might have been six thirty. Maybe six. It was kind of a while ago, you know?"

Hmm, thought Bethesda, and jotted a quick notation

in the margin. *C.P.S.* Call Pirate Sam's.

Natasha yawned and gave Bethesda a tired little smile, and Bethesda thought what a relief it was to have someone reacting to her questions without getting all offended and upset. Natasha didn't look angry at all, in fact, she looked just kind of . . . worn out or something. She was usually the kind of person who spent an hour at the mirror in the morning, putting on lip gloss, trying different earrings, texting friends to find out what they were wearing. Today she was just the slightest bit of a mess: her shirt was rumpled, her skin a little pale, her eyes shadowed with dark circles. The dark red of her nails looked faded and chipped in spots.

"Hey, um, Natasha?" Bethesda asked softly. "Are you doing okay?"

Natasha shrugged. "I guess. I don't know."

A leaf drifted down from the oak tree and settled in Natasha's hair, but she didn't seem to notice. Bethesda reached over and brushed it away.

"Is this"—Bethesda leaned forward slightly—"about Todd?"

There was a pause before Natasha replied—and it's a funny thing about that particular pause. If you had asked Bethesda Fielding if she was asking Natasha about Todd as part of her duties as a semi-official private investigator, or just to be a nice person, she would have selected option B. She was friends with Natasha (well, sort of friends), and she *was* just being a nice person. The girl was obviously a little out of sorts, and it had been pretty clear for the last couple days—couple weeks, now that Bethesda thought about it—that there was something weird going on between her and her old friend Todd.

So she *was* asking to be nice. But all the same, Bethesda's foot—which often had better instincts than she did—was tapping a rapid, enthusiastic bippity-bop against the metal base of the picnic table. Her foot in its Chuck Taylor sneaker clearly thought that the innocent, friendly question she'd put to Natasha was relevant to her ongoing investigation.

It didn't matter, because Natasha didn't answer. She was distracted by a bird.

It was the blue-and-green swallow, hopping in a crook of the fat old oak tree that oversaw the outdoor seating area. As Bethesda watched, Natasha's gaze drifted up to where the bird nestled in its branch, and her face glowed with tenderness. Then she waved at the bird, almost as if they were old friends.

"Hey, buddy," said Natasha to the bird, in such a sweet and simple way that Bethesda said it too. "Hey, buddy."

The bird tilted its tiny head and chittered politely to

Natasha and Bethesda in reply. Then the five-minute bell rang, and all three of them went on their way.

There was, alas, no time left for mystery solving that day. Bethesda had been a total slacker on the weather-phenomenon project for Mr. Darlington's class, and all of a sudden it was due tomorrow. Victor Glebe, sweetly, acted like *he* was the one who'd been a jerk—he told her he'd finish the diorama, and if she'd just come up with something for the in-class presentation, they'd be even steven. Bethesda thanked him copiously, and put aside her investigation that night to concentrate on a Flash Flood Fact Wheel of Fun ("Take a Turn! Spin the Wheel! Learn About Sudden and Rapid Torrents of Rain or River Water!") And their presentation in Science the next day ended up totally great, with Mr. Darlington clapping vigorously for their efforts—as he did for Natasha, Pamela, and Reenie's group, who gave an emotional description of how windstorms affect migrating falcons; and for Todd and Tucker, who performed a rap Todd had written about a baby eagle dying in a mudslide.

Man, Bethesda thought, *what is it with birds around here lately?*

32

It's in the Bag

That night, in her unglamorous high-rise condominium apartment, clad in her favorite fuzzy slippers and sipping tea from her favorite mug, Ida Finkleman was having trouble getting her work done. Staring at her from her dining-room table was the score of the *West Side Story* overture, which her sixth graders would somehow need to master in time for the winter concert. And those quiz questions—there remained a mountain of quiz questions to write.

But instead of doing any of this, Ms. Finkleman booted up her laptop and checked her email. Impatiently she scanned her inbox: an email from her mother about her plans for Thanksgiving; one from her sister Clementine recommending a Tom Waits album, and asking if there was something by Brahms she could recommend in turn.

Nothing from Mr. Ivan Piccolini-Provokovsky of St. Louis, Missouri.

She quickly answered her emails ("still not sure" to her mother, "violin concerto in D" to her sister), stirred a half teaspoonful of sugar into her mug of tea, and picked up her pen to write some quiz questions.

She teased herself for being so disappointed. It had only been a week, after all.

On the other hand, time was running out fast. It was now Wednesday night, and the children were meant to leave for their trip bright and early on Monday morning. Ms. Finkleman turned back to her laptop and typed in the website where she knew she would find the "Save Taproot Valley" video. She watched it and found it to be completely delightful, just as she had the last six times she'd watched it. She sang along with the chorus, clapped for the big dance sections, and chortled merrily when the bear fell down the stairs.

As she was watching, Ms. Finkleman scrolled down to see how the video was doing.

"Two hundred and twelve page views? That's *it*?!"

It was beyond Ms. Finkleman's understanding how Chester's comic masterpiece could be faring so poorly in the great viewing marketplace of the internet, especially when compared with all the clichéd videos of gurgling babies and kittens behaving in an un-kittenlike manner. "Okay, so the cat can drive a riding lawnmower," Ms. Finkleman protested to the empty room. "That deserves 450,000 page views?"

The video ended. She really ought to get to work preparing those quizzes. Instead she clicked back over to her email and hit Compose. Surely it couldn't hurt to follow up.

"Two-hundred and thirteen page views? That's *it*?"

Chester was devastated. He clicked Refresh and groaned. After being online for forty-five and a half hours (not that he was counting or anything), "Save Taproot Valley" had been viewed 213 times, and raised a grand total of $316, twenty bucks of which Chester had contributed himself.

"It's so good, though!" Chester wailed, holding his head between his hands. "It's so funny!"

Didn't the universe recognize a brilliant piece of video art when it saw one? If an eighth-grade boy in a bear costume tumbling down a flight of stairs doesn't deserve overnight-internet-sensation status, what does?

"Chester! Dinner!"

Chester was at his mom's that week, and normally he liked to listen to her stories about her workday, because his mom was a trauma surgeon, and a lot of her stories were really gross. But today he only pretended to listen, feigning interest in the gory details of a tibia repair while he did math in his head: 316 dollars, divided by 45.5 hours, is right around 7 dollars an hour. Okay, so 7 an hour, times 24 hours in a day . . .

Oh crud, thought Chester, coughing on a mouthful of beef. *Crud!*

"Chester? Are you okay?"

"Yeah. Fine."

"Are you sure?" His mom looked a little disappointed, as if she had really been hoping to perform the Heimlich maneuver.

At this rate it would take them about seven hundred hours to raise the money. That was like a month—and they had five *days* until Monday morning, when the buses were supposed to pull up in the horseshoe driveway and take them to Taproot Valley. After dinner, Chester retreated back to his room and hit Refresh. Two more people had watched the movie, and neither had donated anything. One was his Cousin Ilene, who wrote

"Great job!" in the comments section; whoever the other person was, they commented that a chicken costume would have been funnier.

Maybe Victor was right, thought Chester, brushing his teeth for bed. *Maybe this was a stupid plan all along.*

Bethesda lay in bed, clutching Ted-Wo and trying to sleep, watching dark shadows drift and blend on her ceiling. She'd had a frustrating couple of days, starting with the mysterious attack on her poor defenseless bike. She'd gotten no real information from Natasha. When she called Pirate Sam's, the manager (whose name was Stanley but who asked to be addressed as "Squid Guts") had no idea whether the Ficker and Belinsky families had eaten there that Monday, let alone what time. He'd taken down Bethesda's number and said the waiter for that section, Old Filthy Beard, would call her back. Meanwhile, she'd heard nothing new from Tenny—in fact, she'd barely seen her right-hand man this week at all.

She kicked her legs out from under the blanket, then fluffed and refluffed her pillow. Nine suspects danced in the air above her head, popping up one by one like on the opening credits of a TV show. The clues circled and cycled in her mind: the shattered glass and the drops of blood . . . the tiny screw on the floor of the Alcove . . . a batch of copied keys . . . two mysterious singers and their mysterious song. . . .

What about the suspects she hadn't talked to yet? Could Mr. Ferrars have done it himself? Maybe he told her about the keys to keep suspicion from falling on himself?

So many questions and still no answers—the trophy was still missing. But Bethesda knew it was more than Pamela's gymnastics trophy keeping her awake. Sometimes Tenny was around, totally helping, other times he was nowhere to be found, or so distracted and in his head that he might as well be. Then there was Reenie Maslow, and the case of the friendship that ought to be, but wasn't.

It's like . . . it's like everything is missing. Everything . . .

. . . and then Bethesda was strolling through Pilverton Mall, past Pirate Sam's, past the nail salon and the bracelet store, and out onto the beach. *The beach?*

There went Ms. Pinn-Darvish, her jet-black hair bundled under a swim cap, walking her potbellied pig on a leash, his trotters splashing in and out of the breakers. Bethesda waved and kept walking, following a little hopping bird, a bluish swallow. She nearly ran into Todd and Natasha, both dressed for scuba diving. Boney Bones was sunbathing, reading a magazine, with Mr. Darlington beside him. Bethesda's foot traced a ladder of shells, and when she looked up, there was Tenny, his ripped jeans dampened by the spray, his head bobbing up and down to whatever was on his iPod.

"You gotta hear this!" he called, holding out the earbuds to her. "It's in the bag!"

"Who's that by?"

"No, no!" he said, laughing, pointing at the backpack slung over her right shoulder. (Why did she have her backpack at the beach?) "It's in the bag! It's *in the bag.*"

Bethesda's eyes shot open. She sat up in her bed and stared at the clock: *2:45 a.m.*

It's in the bag.

She jumped out of bed, ran to her backpack, and tugged furiously at the zipper. She dumped the contents of the little front pocket on the floor of her room. She sifted through old Post-it notes, assignment sheets, and gum wrappers until she found what she was looking for.

"Of course!" she shouted, then clamped her hand over her mouth and whispered instead. *"Of course!"*

The dingy, off-white piece of plastic lay on the carpet

of her room, and now Bethesda knew it for what it was—a clue. She opened her Sock-Snow notebook and wrote furiously, to be sure she didn't forget any of this before going back to sleep—though she seriously doubted whether she'd be able to sleep at all.

Finally, she'd cracked a piece of the mystery!

33

A Scrape, Then a Bang, and Then a Crash

Suspect #8: Mr. Darlington

Bethesda stopped at the intersection of Hallway A and the Front Hall, at the door of the science room, shifting the small piece of plastic back and forth in her hands.

"Watch out, mystery," she said to herself, and pushed open the door without stopping to knock. "Here I come."

Mr. Darlington was hunched over his desk with a handful of coffee-shop napkins, desperately mopping up a puddle of spilled paste. "Bethesda? Hi. Having a bit of a . . . oh, for heaven's . . ."

The paste was oozing toward the edge of the desk, seeping down the far side, even as it began to dry in crusty ripples along the surface. "I'm constructing a scale model of the Great Barrier Reef . . . undersea tectonics . . . ugh . . ." A dribble of paste smudged his palm. "If you could hand me . . ."

Bethesda fetched Mr. Darlington an oversized roll of paper towels from the sink, and then stood with her hands clasped behind her back, waiting. As he unspooled great handfuls of paper towel and corralled the creeping pool of paste, she felt like a teacher, standing patiently with a grim expression until everyone was paying attention.

At last he finished and looked up at her. "Okay. There we are. Now, what can I do for you?"

Bethesda Fielding, Master Detective, cut right to the chase. "Mr. Darlington, why did you lie to me?"

Mr. Darlington's eyes widened behind his thick glasses. "Go ahead and kick the door shut, will you, Bethesda?"

She did, and then dragged a student chair into place across the desk from him; Bethesda's expression remained steely, but her heart was hammering in her chest. She balanced her notebook carefully on a non-paste-smeared corner of the desk, and listened to what Mr. Darlington now swore to be the truth.

"It *is* true that I was here that Monday after school. It

is true that I was dismantling Mary Bot Lincoln, and for exactly the reason I told you. Principal Van Vreeland said that since Pamela won the big gymnastics trophy, there would no longer be space in the Achievement Alcove to show off the robot that my sixth graders and I had worked so hard on.

"But I wasn't here from after school until four. My wife, Nancy, had dropped me off that morning. She needs the car on Mondays and Wednesdays because she goes to the gym those days. She used to go near our house, but they changed the time of the yoga class. So she found a class at a different gym, but that teacher does Bikram yoga, and Nancy prefers Ashtanga yoga. They're similar in certain ways, although—"

"Mr. Darlington? Stay on target."

"Right. So, the point is, I didn't have the car at school that day, and I needed it to crate up Mary Bot Lincoln and carry her home. You can't carry seventy-nine pieces of disassembled android on a city bus, Bethesda," he said, nervously twisting a crusted piece of paper towel. "So I got a ride from Mr. Melville, then came back later with my car and let myself in."

"With the key that Mr. Ferrars had given you."

Mr. Darlington's eyebrows shot up behind his glasses.

"I can see I'm not the only one who has crumbled before your powers of interrogation."

Bethesda beamed inwardly at the compliment, but managed to keep her serious mystery-solving expression in place. "So, how late were you *really* here that Monday afternoon?"

"I'd say from about five to . . . I don't know. Maybe quarter to six."

Quarter to six. Bingo.

"And during *that* time, did you see or hear anything unusual?"

"Well . . ." Mr. Darlington made a puzzled face. "I *might have.* I might have heard like a, like a *scraping* noise in the hall."

A scrape? Ms. Pinn-Darvish had heard a bang, and then a crash. But a scrape?

"When, Mr. Darlington?"

"What?"

"You said you left at about quarter to six. Did you hear the scrape right around then, or was it earlier? Try to remember. It's important."

He took his glasses off and rubbed his eyes.

"No. No, the scrape was earlier. Around five fifteen or so?" As he put his glasses back on, Bethesda noticed little specks of paste he'd ground into his eyebrows.

"Bethesda, I promise you I did not steal that trophy. I only fudged the truth a bit because . . . well . . ."

"Because you left the door propped open."

Mr. Darlington sighed. "Exactly. I had to make so many trips, getting all those robot parts to my car, that for about a half hour I left the front door jammed open. And I feel terrible about it. I do. I even went to Principal Van Vreeland to try to tell her. But before I could, she started wailing about how she's always wanted a trophy, how sad this is for her . . . and then something about hating Christmas. I'm not sure how that was related. But how could I tell her that this whole thing may have been my fault?"

Bethesda reflected, just as she had when Mr. Ferrars first told her about the keys, how Principal Van Vreeland's fury over the missing trophy was foiling her own desire to get it back. Instead of pressuring the truth out of people, she was terrifying everyone into silence.

"Well, thanks for telling me the truth, Mr. Darlington."

"Better late than never, I suppose." He sighed ruefully and reached for his ocean floor. "Now can I ask *you* a question?"

"Sure."

"How did you know about the door?"

Bethesda smiled and handed over the small off-white piece of plastic, the random little artifact she'd stuffed in the front pocket of her backpack almost a month earlier—before the assembly, before the stolen trophy, before this whole thing began.

"Well, I'll be darned," Mr. Darlington marveled.

He took back the little broken-off piece of Boney Bones's left shin, which he had used to prop open the door, and began pasting it back in place.

Bethesda zoomed down Hallway A toward the back stairwell, walking as fast as she could to the eighth-grade lockers. She was dying to find Tenny before school started so she could fill him in on what she'd learned. Galloping up the stairs, two at a time, she went over the timeline in her head:

1. After school, two people are in the music room, singing . . .
2. Sometime around 5:15, there's a mysterious scraping noise . . .
3. At 5:45, Mr. Darlington kicks shut the front door, causing a loud bang . . .

4. A moment later there's a crashing sound, presumably from the smashing of the trophy case . . .
5. And then the crook does . . . *something* that scatters around the loose pieces of glass, leaving behind
   a. red dots that might or might not be blood,
   b. a tiny screw that might or might not be a clue, and
   c. no trophy!

But why? Bethesda asked herself for the millionth time.

And how?

And, most important, who? Of the suspects on Jasper's key list, only . . .

Bethesda gasped and stopped so suddenly at the top of the stairs that she almost tumbled backward. The list? The list didn't matter anymore! If Mr. Darlington had propped open the door, *the trophy thief didn't need a key!*

All of Bethesda's and Tenny's work—all the carefully annotated index cards, all their ingenious feats of detection, all their bravery and determination—it was all moot. The thief could have been anyone!

Bethesda staggered the last twenty feet to the eighth-grade lockers in a state of shock, her eyes traveling at random to different people, every single one of them a suspect.

Maybe it was Anju, the really tall seventh-grade girl who Violet hung out with!

Maybe it was Mr. Muhammed, the technologies teacher with the rumpled sweaters and the BlackBerry clipped to his belt!

Maybe it was Suzie! Or Shelly! Or both of them together!

Bethesda continued to her locker in a daze, trying to rally, to recover her focus. But the nightmare wasn't over yet. As soon as she touched the dial of the lock, before she even twisted the combination to the first number, the metal door of her locker began to creep slowly open on its own. Bethesda stumbled back and watched, astonished, as the door swung out.

Bethesda brought her hands up to her mouth, stunned. Other kids gathered around, gaping. "Whoa!" she heard Rory mutter. "Oh my god," Bessie whispered softly.

Inside Bethesda's locker was a taunting riot of color, like an overturned spaghetti bowl of blues and greens and reds, twisting and overlapping in a dense, squishy tangle. *Silly String!* Someone had broken into her locker and filled it with Silly String. Her magazine clippings, her heart-shaped mirror, her stack of school supplies cases, her little Benjamin Franklin action figure, all buried in yards and yards of Silly String.

And there, folded into careful eighths and nested in the sticky web of Silly String, was a note.

I FIRMLY REITERATE MY EARLIER INSISTENCE THAT YOU TERMINATE YOUR IMPERTINENT INQUIRIES!

And then, lower down, in slightly smaller letters:

(SORRY ABOUT YOUR LOCKER.)

While her fellow eighth graders buzzed around her, slamming closed their lockers and racing off to first period, Bethesda let the note drop from her hand and flutter to the ground. Whoever this mysterious, fancy-word-slinging bandit was, whoever was so determined that she fail, they were in luck.

Because Bethesda wasn't even close.

34

The Very Short Interrogation of Ida Finkleman

Suspect #8: Ms. Finkleman

As Bethesda's conversation with Mr. Darlington unfolded, Tenny was over in Hallway C, conducting his own final suspect interrogation. It was a pretty fast interrogation.

"Hey, so, Ms. Finkleman. Did you take the trophy?"

"No. I didn't."

"Okay, cool."

This was Ms. Finkleman we were talking about. She listened to Radiohead, and could play a halfway decent rhythm guitar—her word was good enough for Tenny. Besides, his heart wasn't really in this whole detective thing today. Even though he really ought to hit his locker before first period, he lingered in the Band and Chorus room, wandering around while Ms. Finkleman sat at her desk, writing quiz questions and occasionally checking her laptop. In the tall instrument cabinet, Tenny discovered an old mandolin and began to experiment, teaching his fingers to find chords on the tiny little frets.

Yesterday, after Social Studies, Tucker Wilson had asked him if it was true that he'd been tossed out of St. Francis Xavier because he drove the headmaster's car into Lake Vaughn. He'd mumbled something about how stupid that was, but Tucker looked unconvinced. Whatever. It wasn't any of that kid's business. It wasn't *anyone's* business. Tenny eased back into a chair, playing a high-octave version of the Nirvana song "Smells Like Teen Spirit" on the mandolin.

Then, with only a minute or two left until first period, Ms. Finkleman looked up from her desk and embarked very gently on a conversation—the same conversation they'd been having, once every few days, for the last two weeks.

"So? Tenny? How are you doing?"

"Um . . . all right. Good days and bad days, ya know?" He paused, coughed. "Today's not so hot."

"Well." She shrugged, smiled. "If you need anything . . ."

He nodded, said, "See ya," and was gone.

This brief conversation didn't feel like much to Ms. Finkleman. But if there was one thing she had learned from a lifetime in music—coaxing the right rush of notes from a violin, subtly working the pedals of a piano—sometimes a little bit is all you need.

35

Things You're Not Supposed to Know

"So there is going to be seventh-grade stuff, plus everything we've done so far this year. Got it, people?"

In first period, Ms. Fischler was handing out the testing schedule for next week. Monday, percentage/fraction conversion. Tuesday, algebraic inequalities. Wednesday, she promised, "will be kind of the easy day. We'll just be mapping binomials, so bring your graphing calculators."

In second period, Dr. Capshaw announced that they'd be suspending their progress through *Animal Farm* until after the quiz week, since they'd have no time for class discussions, anyway.

"But we want to know what happens," said Ellis Walters.

"I'm sorry," said Dr. Capshaw. "But you are of course welcome to read ahead on your own."

"Like we'll have time," grumbled Ellis.

It was like this all over school. Everybody had thought that, somehow, the Week of a Thousand Quizzes wouldn't really happen. The trophy thief would confess, or be caught; Principal Van Vreeland would, miraculously, change her mind; a tornado would come out of nowhere, lift up the whole school in the middle of the night, and carry it out to sea. Alas, nothing of the sort had occurred, and now, with the dreaded week of testing four days away, Principal Van Vreeland had succeeded in her goal: everybody in the entire school was as miserable and angry as she was. (Except Mr. Melville, whose constant whistling wasn't helping matters in the least.)

Adding to the general funk was the fact that it was the second Thursday of the month, and that was fish-stick day. By the time the lunch bell rang, the queasy smell of deep-fried cod was drifting out of the cafeteria and suffusing the whole school. Just inside the cafeteria doors, in this thick fog of fish-stick smell, Bethesda was pacing, waiting for her sidekick.

"Tenny! Finally!" she yelped as he slouched into the cafeteria.

"Hey," he said absently. "So, uh, I talked to Ms. Finkleman this morning. Yeah, I don't think she did it."

"Doesn't matter," Bethesda said impatiently. She told Tenny about her dream, about the little piece of Boney Bones, about Mr. Darlington and the propped-open door.

"Whoa," he said mildly. Clearly the massiveness of the revelation had barely registered. *Well, terrific*, thought Bethesda. Their investigation was collapsing all around them, and he'd disappeared into one of his fogs of weirdness.

"We can still do this, Tenny, if we focus. The suspect list can't matter *that* much. We have tons of other clues." Urgently, she ticked them off on her hand, trying to fake confidence she didn't feel. "One. The mysterious singers in the Band room. Two, the scattered glass. Three, the red dots. Four . . . the . . . Tenny? Hello?"

She couldn't take it anymore. He was drumming his fingers on the table, puffing out his cheeks, staring off in random directions.

"What's up, Tenny? Are you listening? Not listening? Are you writing songs in your head or something?"

"What? No." He shook his head, made a face. "I'm just thinking."

"About what? *Tenny!*"

Suddenly his spaced-out expression came into sharp focus. "Bethesda, did it ever occur to you there might be other things in the world beside your project?"

"My project?" Bethesda stared back at him. "*Our* project!"

"Okay, so the eighth grade doesn't get to go to Taproot Valley. What's the big deal?"

"What's the big deal?" she echoed, flabbergasted. "God! Tenny, we're supposed to be solving a mystery together, and you're, like, the biggest mystery of all. You suddenly show up from St. Francis Xavier, and you won't even tell me why you got kicked out . . ."

"I didn't get kicked out!"

His shout drew attention from all over the lunchroom. In the suddenly hushed, staring crowd, Tenny drew the hood of his sweatshirt up over his hair and shrank down in his seat.

"Thanks a lot, Bethesda."

"It's not my fault. How was I supposed to know?"

"Did you ever think that there are things you're not supposed to know?"

Tenny sat with arms folded, his eyes blazing from the depths of his hood.

The anger that had been simmering in Bethesda since 8:20 that morning, when she emerged from Mr. Darlington's room and had her gut-wrenching epiphany, now came to full boil. She threw up her arms and stomped past Tenny out of the cafeteria toward the front door of the school.

"Bethesda?" said Tenny, close at her heels. "Where are you going?"

"What do you care?"

Bethesda heard the nastiness in her voice and knew instantly that she'd regret it. But it was too late now. She was a missile heading for its target.

Find the thief? she thought furiously. *Find her? I've known who it was from the very beginning!*

And there was the prime suspect, the real suspect, sitting blithely on a picnic bench, exactly where Bethesda had known she would be—in *Bethesda's* seat, at Bethesda's place, wedged between Shelly and Hayley, her glasses off and folded on the table beside her, her reddish-tannish hair clipped above her ears, a book balanced on her lap. *Always reading,* Bethesda thought disdainfully, *always making sure everyone knows how smart you are.*

IOM. Irene Olivia Maslow.

"I know it was you."

Reenie raised her head slowly and returned Bethesda's stare unflinchingly.

"You know what was me?"

The picnic-tables crowd looked over at the confrontation. Most of them were clustered around a laptop Suzie had checked out from Technologies, watching the "Save Taproot Valley" video for the zillionth time. Suzie hit a button, the movie paused on a shot of Braxton with paws outstretched, and everyone's attention turned to the strange sight of Bethesda Fielding glowering at Reenie Maslow.

"You're the one who stole Pamela's trophy."

In all the mystery books, in all the movies, when the hero swoops in to unmask her nefarious adversary, there's always this dramatic confrontation, where the bad guy either makes a break for it, or begs for mercy. Bethesda took a big dramatic step backward, waiting for one of those things to happen. But Reenie neither sprinted toward Friedman Street nor fell pleadingly to her knees. Instead she carefully picked up her glasses off the picnic bench, unfolded the stems to put them on, and said, "No I didn't."

Bethesda blinked.

"Yes you did."

"No I didn't."

"Yes you *did*!"

Bethesda was feeling less like a world-class detective unmasking her diabolical foe, and more like a kindergartner fighting in a sandbox.

"All right, let's all just calm down here," said Chester Hu, rising from his place beside Suzie and stepping toward them, waving his hands for calm. "Bethesda, why do you think Reenie did it?"

"Excellent question!" Bethesda replied, thrusting a finger into the air. In her most resonant, closing-argument voice, Bethesda revealed the powerful evidence she had kept hidden for so long. "In the Achievement Alcove, behind the trophy case, I found three little initials written on the base of the back wall. IOM! As in Irene Olivia Maslow!"

Bethesda stepped backward and crossed her arms: Case closed.

The problem was, no one looked all that convinced.

"Wait—*IOM*?" asked Pamela, wrinkling her nose with confusion. "Wouldn't she have signed it *ROM*? Everyone calls her Reenie."

"I was thinking the same thing," added Suzie, and

Shelly nodded in agreement.

"Actually," Bessie Stringer threw in, "Why would she sign it at all?"

"Good point," said Ezra.

"Well . . . I don't know!" Bethesda sputtered. "Ask *her*!"

But Reenie said nothing. She just sat there and looked at Bethesda, her face blank.

"Also, IOM could stand for a lot of stuff," put in Rory, smoothing his long black hair with one hand. "Like Ireland's only mountain. Or interesting oily monkeys."

Bethesda sighed in frustration. "You guys, come on! Reenie did it! It's so *obvious*."

Marisol Pierce looked at Bethesda. "I don't know. It doesn't really seem all that obvious."

"Yeah," Pamela agreed. She made a sour, skeptical face. "Why would Reenie steal my trophy?"

"Because . . . ," Bethesda started, and then stopped and glanced quickly at Reenie, who sat still and cold as a statue.

"Well, for a lot of reasons."

"Name one."

"Well . . . to . . . um . . ."

"Iggy oinked merrily!" Rory shouted suddenly.

"Good one," said Ezra, and slapped him five.

Suzie started the video again, and everyone turned back to Braxton's classic pratfall, already in progress. Bethesda stood helplessly, her hands flapping at her sides. Just like that, her big dramatic moment had passed.

Except that, suddenly, Reenie turned and addressed her with a voice coiled tightly as a striking snake. "Bethesda, I am very sorry that your little investigation didn't work out as you planned it," she said. "But that doesn't mean you should go around blaming people just because you happen to dislike them."

"Dislike you?" Bethesda was stunned. "I don't dislike you! You dislike *me*!"

"I don't dislike you. I barely *know* you." Reenie stepped carefully around Bethesda, chucked her empty lunch bag in the garbage, and walked toward the door of the school.

"Wait!" Bethesda shouted. She knew she was right and she knew she could prove it. "Wait!"

Suzie paused the movie again, this time on one of the innumerable Pamela Preston close-ups. Reenie stopped at the door, shaking her head sadly, like she was the mature one, tolerating Bethesda's childish behavior out of sheer pity.

"Pamela's trophy was stolen from the Achievement

Alcove at approximately five forty-five on Monday the twentieth," Bethesda announced, then pointed dramatically at Reenie. "What were you doing at five forty-five that day?"

"I . . . well . . . Mondays . . ." Reenie thought for a moment, and then her cool-as-a-cucumber attitude abruptly disappeared. Her face got red and she stared at Bethesda with open hostility. "That's none of your business!"

"Aha!" said Bethesda. All the eighth graders leaned in closer, except Pamela, who snuck a quick admiring glance at her freeze-framed face on the screen. "If Reenie wasn't stealing the trophy, she'd tell us where she was!"

"Bethesda, no offense, but I'm, like, totally sure you're wrong," said Natasha, speaking up for the first time. "Reenie, why don't you just tell us what you were doing. Then Bethesda will know she made a mistake."

"Fine. I was . . . I . . . ," Reenie began, and then stopped and cleared her throat. She looked caught and helpless, like a mouse in the jaws of a trap. Bethesda felt a fleeting rush of sympathy, quickly drowned in a wave of anticipation. Her moment of triumph was at hand! Bethesda Fielding, Master Detective, would be the hero after all!

"I was at home, with my tutor."

"Tutor? Why would *you* need a tutor?"

Reenie looked straight up in the air, took a deep breath, and returned her gaze to Bethesda. "Because I'm way, way behind."

Bethesda scrunched up her face. "Behind? In what subject?"

"All of them."

Bethesda's heart lurched in her chest. *Oh, no.*

"But . . . but you're so smart. You're always reading. Trying to get ahead."

Reenie let out a small, rueful laugh. "Get ahead? Hardly. I'm just trying to keep up."

"But why didn't you just tell everyone that?"

"Why didn't I tell everyone?" Reenie laughed again, shaking her head. "If everyone thought you were some sort of genius, and actually they were completely wrong, would you tell them?"

Bethesda opened her mouth and then shut it again. The crowd at the picnic tables was hushed and still. Suzie's computer went dark and the school's official screen saver came up, an image of Mary Todd Lincoln wearing a Bluetooth headset. Looking helplessly around the picnic benches, Bethesda's eyes landed on Tenny, who wore an expression of total disgust—an expression, she knew, that had nothing to do with fish sticks.

36

I Know What I've Got to Do

"Hey, Bethesda? Someone named Old Filthy Beard called for you."

"Oh. Okay."

School was over. Bethesda was sprawled lengthwise on the couch with her face squashed into the pillows, staring into the rumpled green fabric. Her dad was shuttling back and forth to the kitchen, putting the finishing touches on his chili, preparing to knock the socks off everyone at the law firm charity dinner that night. He paused, leaning into the living room from the kitchen door, his chef's hat at a rakish angle.

"He said . . . hold on, let me get this right." Bethesda's father put on a respectable pirate voice to deliver the message. "'Aye, those fam'lies were here on that Monday evenin', at six bells, and no doubtin' it, matey. Every one of 'em, just as always, tho' the wee lassie arrived late as usual.'"

"Okay, Dad. Thanks."

So Natasha and Guy's alibis held up. Big whoop. Bethesda wasn't in the mood to think about the mystery. She wasn't in the mood, in fact, to think about anything at all. She basically spent the next four hours on the couch, eating but not really tasting the pizza she ordered for dinner. She did a little studying for the upcoming blizzard of quizzes, flipping through her math notes, scanning a couple chapters of *The Last Full Measure*. She turned on music but turned it off right away. All the songs she liked reminded her of Tenny, and of all the things she didn't feel like thinking about, she felt like thinking about Tenny least of all.

When her parents got home, she was still on the sofa. "Well?" she said, muting the episode of *You're Going to Wear That?* she was sort of watching. Her father didn't answer, and her mother shook her head sadly as she plopped down next to Bethesda on the sofa. "What happened?"

"Everybody went crazy for Marilyn Sokal's spare ribs, is what happened," said Bethesda's father glumly. "They were the big hit of the night."

"Only because she's a partner, honey," said Bethesda's mom.

"Really?"

"Of course, sweetheart. Yours was the best. No question."

After Bethesda's father went upstairs, they sat quietly for a moment or two, Bethesda's mom easing out of her pinchy black work shoes, Bethesda turning something over in her head.

"Mom? Was Dad's really the best?"

Her mom shot a quick look at the stairs. "Well . . . let's just say sometimes you have to bend the truth a little bit, if that's what doing the right thing requires. Know what I mean, baby doll?"

When she was alone again, an image appeared in Bethesda's mind, as vivid as if she were watching it on a 3-D screen: Chester Hu outside the Main Office, standing perfectly still with his hand at the doorknob, summoning the courage to stride in there and face Serious, Permanent-Record Big Trouble, just to save Taproot Valley for Marisol Pierce and the others. Chester, his head in a muddle but his heart swollen by a sense of nobility, preparing to sacrifice himself for the greater good.

Bethesda Fielding rose from the sofa. She knew what she had to do.

Meanwhile, in a house across town, a pair of eyes was once again staring deeply into a mirror in the upstairs bathroom. "I know what I've got to do." The eyes peered searchingly at their reflected image, as if the mirrored glass could reveal not just a face, but a *soul*. "I know what I've got to do."

"What? Did you say something in there, hon?"

"No! *God!*"

There was a third person who was up late that night with worry. Reenie Maslow, faced with the prospect of the Week of a Thousand Quizzes, was studying even more than usual these days—by herself, with her tutor, with her mother, with her older sister. All she did was study. Even now, long after the rest of the family had gone to sleep, she was studying, flipping again and again through her flashcards on binomials. But it was useless. Her mind kept replaying that afternoon, at the picnic benches. And that Friday afternoon, at the library . . . and the time on their bikes . . .

It wasn't going to be fun. But Reenie knew what she had to do.

37

A Confession to Make

"**I** have a confession to make."

Bethesda stood at the mirror, practicing the words she would say in the principal's office, and how she would say them.

"I have a confession to make."

She tried saying it slowly and quietly, with head down and chin very slightly quivering, as if on the brink of tears. "I have . . . a . . . confession . . . to . . . to . . . make . . ."

She tried saying it really, really fast, the awful truth bursting forth like water from a dam. "Ihaveaconfessiontomake!"

She tried saying the words boldly and proudly, standing upright and squaring her shoulders, as if making not a shocking admission, but a valiant declaration. "I have a confession to make!"

Ultimately Bethesda decided to keep it simple. She would calmly explain to Principal Van Vreeland that it was she, Bethesda Fielding, who broke the trophy case and stole Pamela Preston's trophy. And then she would suffer what would surely be a wide-ranging and diverse menu of consequences. Watching on Monday morning as everyone went off to Taproot Valley without her would be just the beginning.

Bethesda had sworn she'd catch the crook and save the trip. She had failed the first part, but she could come through on the second: she'd take the blame so the rest of the kids could go. She fixed her hair in black barrettes and smoothed her purple dress. (She'd decided to dress all in black, then discovered that her only black skirt was from an old witch costume, and decided purple was close enough).

"I have a confession to make," she said, one last time, then trudged off to school and certain doom.

"Bethesda! Bethesda!"

She halted, mid-trudge. Who was that?

"I have a confession to make!"

She was at the corner of Friedman and Devonshire, T minus ten minutes from certain-doom time, when she heard the wild and desperate voice that was shouting her name. And saying her line.

"I have a confession to make!"

It was Victor Glebe, running toward her down Friedman Street in big, ungainly strides, his glasses slipping down the bridge of his nose. He caught up to Bethesda and stood panting at her side for a long moment, slightly hunched over, breathing hard.

"It was . . . it was *me*, Bethesda," Victor managed at last. "I did it. I'm . . ." Victor took one last heaving breath and straightened up. "I'm so sorry."

Bethesda rocked on the balls of her feet, her mind alight. Her purple dress rippled lightly in the gentle fall breeze.

Victor did it! I don't have to fake-confess!

Taproot Valley is saved!

A last-minute coup from Master Detective Bethesda Fielding! And the crowd goes wild!

There was just one question. "Victor, why would you steal Pamela's trophy?"

"Huh?" Victor squinted at Bethesda, confused. "No. No! I didn't do *that*."

Argle bargle.

"So, what are you confessing to?"

"I'm your inscrutable tormentor." Bethesda looked back at him, confused. "Your unfathomable adversary? Wreathed in shadow?"

"What?"

Victor sighed. "I'm the one who filled your locker with Silly String, Bethesda. And I let the air out of your bicycle tires. I wrote those notes. I'm really sorry." Victor produced a heavily dog-eared student-edition *Roget's Thesaurus* from his backpack. "And remorseful. And contrite. And compunctious."

"I get it!"

Bethesda snatched away the thesaurus, resisting the urge to toss it in the gutter. Bethesda had been friends, or at least friendly acquaintances, with Victor Glebe since they were seven years old, and had never known him to be anything but quiet, serious, and rigorously polite. She certainly didn't think him the type to commit petty acts of vandalism, or go around threatening people. "Why would you do that?"

"Because I'm scared of the dark, Bethesda."

"What?"

"And snakes. And horses. I really don't like horses."

"So, you mean . . . oh, Victor. Seriously?"

Bethesda's irritation softened. She imagined what

Victor must have been going through these last few weeks. What he must have been going through since they entered Mary Todd Lincoln as sixth graders, two years ago, and people started talking about Taproot Valley. What a relief it must have been for the long-dreaded week of outdoor education suddenly to be canceled. And here she was, trying to get it un-canceled!

"Oh, and bonfires," Victor went on. "I really don't like bonfires. One stray twig flies off, and *poof*, the whole forest is toast."

"Hey, Victor, you know what?" said Bethesda. "It's okay." As annoying as Victor's underhanded efforts had been, this morning she had bigger fish to fry. Bethesda resumed her trudge to school, with a remorseful Victor Glebe now trailing along beside her. Soon they reached the horseshoe driveway, just a few feet from the front doors. In the cool early-morning sun, Mary Todd Lincoln Middle School loomed massive and stark as a jail.

"Ah!" Suddenly, Victor tossed his hands up in front of his face and stumbled backward.

"What's the matter?"

"That bird! It'll peck our eyes out!"

It was the blue-green swallow, Natasha's little buddy, chirping merrily in the arm of the fat oak. Bethesda sighed and patted Victor on the arm. This was one kid who did not need a week in the woods.

"I have a confession to make."

Okay, Bethesda thought. *Now this is getting ridiculous.*

This time it was Reenie Maslow, shifting uneasily from one foot to the other. She had stopped Bethesda right outside the Main Office, right where Bethesda had stopped Chester, four weeks and a lifetime ago.

Reenie stared uneasily at Bethesda, hands hanging nervously at her sides.

I was right! thought Bethesda with astonishment, turning away from the door. *I was right all along!*

"Don't get all excited," Reenie said pointedly. "I *still* didn't steal Pamela's stupid trophy."

"Oh."

Argle bargle. Again.

"But I do have a confession to make. Bethesda, I—"

"Ha! Ha!"

The booming laugh, echoing like cannon fire from the far end of the Front Hall, belonged to Coach Vasouvian, no doubt cracking up over some deeply sarcastic comment from Mr. Melville, who walked beside him. At the sound of it, Reenie jumped a little, and Bethesda instinctively reached out and placed a steadying hand on her shoulder. Suddenly Reenie seemed very small and helpless, a baby bird lost in the vast hallway. Bethesda pictured the school as it would be in a few minutes, overflowing with rambunctious students and scowling teachers, kids banging against each other and trading insults, flitting in and out of their various cliques and clans, flicking rubber bands, shouting and teasing and flirting. Such an environment must be difficult for someone new, especially someone as inward and reserved as Reenie Maslow.

"Here. This way," said Bethesda, grasping Reenie by the arms and pulling her into the safe harbor of the Achievement Alcove. They squatted together with their backs to the wall, in the rear left corner, right beneath Marisol Pierce's prize-winning charcoal drawing.

"So, what's going on, Reenie?"

Reenie stared at the floor of the Achievement Alcove and spoke very quickly, her words emerging in a mumbly rush. "You were right at lunch yesterday. I *did* dislike you. I've disliked you since we met."

"Okay." Bethesda leaned away from Reenie, pushing farther back against the wall of the alcove. "Why?"

"Because you're smart. And people like you."

"Are you kidding? Everyone hates me! I'm a walking disaster! I ruined the Taproot Valley trip, remember?"

"Yeah, but that's just right this second. I'm talking all the time. You're always running around, making jokes, trading lunches with people, raising your hand in class. You do every single extracurricular activity."

"No I don't. Just debate, yearbook, newspaper, math team, and peer tutoring."

"That's a lot."

"Oh, and computer club. And swim."

"I guess it's like . . . you know." Reenie shrugged. "I'm always scared that smart people are going to make me feel stupid."

Bethesda groaned. "And then yesterday, that's exactly what I did." Her heart flooded with empathy for Reenie Maslow. This girl was so *not* her nefarious adversary.

"Well, you didn't mean to, I don't think."

"No!" Bethesda said earnestly. "I really didn't."

Bethesda inched closer to Reenie on the grimy floor of the Achievement Alcove. They were making up! They could turn from bitterest enemies to friends! Maybe she could tutor Reenie after school, just like she had tutored Tenny last year. Hey, actually, maybe the three of them could form a band!

Bethesda reached forward with arms extended, and Reenie pulled away.

"Were you going to hug me?"

"What? No." Bethesda's face flared red. "I have this weird arm condition."

"Oh. Well, anyway. I'm sorry I disliked you for no reason."

"I'm sorry, too."

Reenie heaved herself up from the floor of the Alcove, and offered a hand to Bethesda to pull her up, too. "There's this thing my mom always says, about how life is a ladder, and other people are the rungs. If you don't have other people, you'll fall right back down. Cheesy, right?"

"Oh, please," replied Bethesda, shaking her head, as the two girls emerged from the Achievement Alcove. "If you want cheesy, you should hear my dad. He . . ."

Bethesda stopped, her mouth hanging open.

"Bethesda?" said Reenie. "Uh, Bethesda?"

Life is a ladder, Reenie had said. "A ladder!"

Somewhere inside the mind of Bethesda Fielding, Master Detective, wheels were turning, slowly at first, and then faster and faster and faster. Gears were catching on gears, thoughts zinging to and fro, ideas blinking furiously like the lights on a pinball table.

"Our trophy thief would need something a lot harder than a fist to break the glass . . ." That was Tenny Observation #1. Something like the heavy foot of a custodian's ladder.

But . . . why a ladder? Who needed a ladder? You need ladders to reach . . . to reach . . .

Bethesda cried out. "Up! Look up, Reenie! Help me find it."

"Find what? Bethesda, are you okay?"

"The vent! There!"

Reenie craned her neck and saw what Bethesda saw. On the wall above the Achievement Alcove, a slotted metal plate, just a simple air-conditioner vent, but hanging slightly loose, with one tiny screw missing.

"Okay," said Reenie. "So . . ."

"Hold on one sec." Bethesda's mind spun furiously. *Why would someone open that vent? Who . . . who had been obsessed with the vents?*

Janitor Steve! He had tapped his broom handle, tap-tap-tap, against the air ducts; he'd insisted to Tenny that a noisy spirit was in there, or had been until just before the trophy disappeared. But there was no such thing as ghosts, so what was *really* trapped up there? What really needed to be *set free*?

"Holy smoke," Bethesda whispered.

"What?" Reenie said. "*What?*"

Into Bethesda's mind flew the bird. The bird that had terrified poor Victor Glebe that morning. That bird she'd seen hopping along with a scrap of Ding Dong dangling from its beak. The sweet bird, tilting its little head and chittering politely, the morning of her seventh interrogation, as if to say . . . to say *thank you.*

The bird!

"Reenie. I know what happened to that trophy!"

38

Simple Human Decency

After Bethesda gave her explanation to Reenie, they raced together to the Band and Chorus room. There they found both Ms. Finkleman and Tenny, as Bethesda had suspected they might.

"Whoa," said Tenny, when Bethesda revealed who did it, and how. And then, although he was still mad at her about yesterday, Tenny helped her piece together the few details she was still missing—like the exact timing of the scrape, bang, and crash, and where the little red dots came from.

But it was Reenie who came up with the plan, and who convinced an extremely reluctant Band and Chorus teacher to play her part. By the time the first-period bell rang, and Ms. Finkleman's sixth graders filed in, everyone knew what they had to do. By the end of the day, the mystery of the missing trophy would be all wrapped up—unless, of course, the whole thing fell to pieces.

Which, Bethesda warned herself as she trotted off toward Ms. Fischler's room, *there's every chance it might.*

"Silence!" proclaimed Principal Van Vreeland, raising her hands imperiously above her head as she took her place at the lectern.

The command was completely unnecessary. The auditorium was pin-drop silent, especially in the back, where the eighth graders sat, wide-eyed and frozen with tense anticipation. The word had been going around all day that the culprit had been found, and the all-school punishment was—potentially, possibly, hopefully—over. The eighth graders could practically feel the lumpy vinyl seats of the special field-trip bus beneath their butts; they could practically smell the scents of grass and skunk and pine awaiting them at Taproot Valley.

Please, thought Tucker and Ezra and Bessie. *Please,* thought Rory and Lindsey and Lisa. *Please let it be true!*

"Ms. Finkleman, if you would join me on the stage?"

The mousy Band and Chorus teacher walked swiftly up the short steps to the lectern, while a ripple of confused looks passed through the auditorium. What did Ms. Finkleman have to do with all this? Principal Van Vreeland stepped aside and surveyed the audience, literally licking her lips with anticipation of finding out who stole her trophy. Bethesda pushed back a lock of reddish-tannish hair and exchanged nervous glances with Tenny Boyer, slumped a few seats over, and with Reenie Maslow, who flashed her a quick, furtive thumbs-up. *All right, Ms. Finkleman*, Bethesda thought, turning her eyes to the stage. *You can do it.*

"Ah, yes. Good afternoon. Principal Van Vreeland, everyone, I am—uh—I am very disappointed to report that the person who stole the gymnastics trophy is . . ."

Ms. Finkleman paused dramatically. A loud *ker-clunk* reverberated through the room; it was Coach Vasouvian, swinging closed the heavy auditorium door in case the criminal, once unmasked, decided to make a run for it. And then Ms. Finkleman finished her sentence, leveling a finger toward the back of the room:

". . . *Tennyson Boyer.*"

The silence broke: everyone talking at once, everyone gasping and whispering, everyone straining and jostling to get a peek at the thief.

"Wait—Tenny?"

"That spacey kid?"

"Does he even go here anymore?"

"Tenny *Boyer*?"

Teachers shushed the kids, even as they themselves muttered and looked around for Tenny and mouthed "wow" at one another. Pamela Preston, who happened to be sitting right in front of Tenny, whipped around in her seat to glare at him, but Pamela's fury was nothing compared with that of Principal Van Vreeland. Her lips curled as she spat out one short, sharp sentence. "Is that so?"

As for Tenny, Bethesda thought he did an admirable job of looking shocked by the accusation. He shot upright in his seat, blinking furiously, whipping his head this way and that, jabbing a finger into his chest. All in all, an Oscar-worthy pantomime of "Who, *me*?"

"That's right," Ms. Finkleman continued. "Though I wish it weren't so, for young Tennyson is a student I have personally worked closely with, and have always liked. But facts are facts." Ms. Finkleman paused here to shake her head sadly. "It seems he was kicked out of St. Francis Xavier for extreme misbehavior—"

"I *told* you guys!" shouted Tucker Wilson. "I told you it was true about the car in the lake!"

"—which he apparently continued at our school, even before being officially reenrolled."

Here Ms. Finkleman paused and looked directly at Tenny, letting a note of grievous disappointment creep into her voice. "Oh, Tenny, how could you?"

From his seat, Tenny pretended to protest, and Ms. Finkleman pretended to cut him off.

"Don't make it worse by lying, Tenny. *Please.*"

Bethesda found she was getting a little choked up, then had to remind herself the whole thing was a ruse. Bethesda and Reenie had told Ms. Finkleman what to say, and instructed Tenny on how to react, designed the whole thing to be as powerful and emotionally affecting as possible. That way the real guilty parties would feel so bad for Tenny, unjustly accused of the crime that they had committed, they'd have to confess. Simple human decency would demand it!

Bethesda craned her head toward the back row, where the culprits were sitting, saying nothing, staring at Tenny like everyone else. So far, simple human decency was not coming through.

Tenny, meanwhile, pushed his performance to the next level. He leaped from his seat, his thick mass of brown curls bobbing wildly, and spoke pleadingly to Ms.

Finkleman. "But I'm innocent. I swear!"

"That's quite enough, young man." Principal Van Vreeland stepped forward slowly, deliberately, as if so enraged that she had to control her movements, lest she get overexcited and burst into flames. "I'll take it from here."

A shiver chased itself down Bethesda's spine. This was where the plan got a little scary, because this is where it was out of their control. Ms. Finkleman was acting; the furious principal was *not*. Bethesda risked another glance at the culprits. Nothing. *Hello? Simple human decency? Where are you?*

"Look, ma'am, I didn't do it," Tenny protested, sounding increasingly desperate. "I really didn't." But Principal Van Vreeland scoffed at his denials, her voice rising with every word. "You will be expelled from this school. From this *district*! No public school in this county will have you!"

Tenny looked wildly around the auditorium, and Bethesda was pretty sure she saw the moment that his pretend fear had transformed into real, serious fear. She and Reenie exchanged panicky glances. Ms. Finkleman stood on the stage, one hand clapped over her mouth. There was no backup plan. Principal Van Vreeland was going to throw Tenny out of school! What had they done?

"Now where is my trophy, child?" The principal burst into motion, charging down the three little steps at the lip of the stage toward Tenny. Jasper chased her down the aisle, grabbing feebly at her shoulders, but the principal shook him off like a charging horse shakes off a fly.

"I don't know where the trophy is!" Tenny cringed backward, holding up his hands, as Principal Van Vreeland bore down on him. "I swear I don't know!"

Bethesda sent urgent telepathic entreaties to the two culprits, but they were still just sitting there, slack-jawed, eyes glued to the spectacle. *Come on, simple human decency*, Bethesda pleaded. *Come on!*

And then, miraculously . . .

"Stop!" shouted Todd Spolin, jumping out of his seat along the back wall of the auditorium, just as Principal Van Vreeland brought her trembling hands down on Tenny's shoulders.

"Tenny Boyer didn't take that stupid trophy. I did."

"Yeah," said Natasha Belinsky, rising from her own seat. "And I helped."

39

But Where's My Trophy?

"**Y**ou?!"

Principal Van Vreeland released her grip on Tenny Boyer and swiveled her whole body like a satellite dish toward the back of the auditorium. Todd stood at one end of the very last row, Natasha at the other, neither looking at the other. Ms. Finkleman, with obvious relief, retreated from the lectern, stumbled off the stage, and sat heavily in a seat in the front row. "It worked," Bethesda mouthed to Reenie. "It actually worked!" Reenie drew the back of her hand across her forehead: *phew*.

Pamela Preston, meanwhile, was staring with horror at Todd and Natasha, her two best friends. "You guys?" she said, and for once the little tears in her eyes looked real. *"Why?"*

"Oh, Pam . . ." Natasha murmured.

"It's, uh, well," said Todd. He took off his baseball cap and twisted it between his hands. "It's kind of a long story."

"Please," barked Principal Van Vreeland. "We'd all *love* to hear it."

Bethesda had the details pretty much exactly right, although it took Natasha and Todd a lot longer to tell the story than it had for her to tell it to Reenie and the others that morning. This is very likely because Todd and Natasha weren't nearly as excited to reveal the truth as Bethesda had been, and also because they were continually bombarded by enraged interjections from the principal.

The first of these interjections came almost immediately after Todd began.

"So, it was that Monday night about five ten. I was biking past the school, on my way home from karate, and I saw that the door was propped open."

"The door was *what?*"

Mr. Darlington was seated all the way at the front of the room with his seventh-period sixth graders, so Bethesda couldn't nudge him in the ribs or look at him significantly. Turned out she didn't have to.

"If these children can, uh—that is, if they can tell the truth, so can I," said the science teacher, rising to his feet. Looking anywhere but at Principal Van Vreeland, Mr. Darlington explained haltingly how he'd been unloading Mary Bot Lincoln after school, and how he'd made things easier for himself by jamming open the front door. The principal nodded curtly, assuring him that they would discuss the matter in more detail later. "Great," Mr. Darlington replied, sinking slowly back into his seat. "I'll look forward to it."

"Okay, so, anyway," Todd said when the principal gestured for him to continue. "The door was open, and I went inside."

"For what purpose?"

"It's going to sound crazy. To, uh . . ." He shuffled a little and looked at Natasha, who looked at her feet. "To, uh . . ."

Bethesda couldn't take it anymore. "To save a bird that was trapped in the vent!"

Todd and Natasha looked at each other, astonished, and then at Bethesda.

"Oh my god," said Natasha. "How did you know that?"

She knew because she'd seen the little swallow on the

morning after the trophy's disappearance, and had noted to herself that it was the first time it'd been around in a while. She knew because she'd heard the silly song they made up, about setting free the poor trapped animal. She knew because she'd found the tiny screw on the floor of the Alcove, where Todd had accidentally left it behind after unscrewing the vent cover. She knew because she'd observed both of them, in the weeks since, paying special attention to the sweet blue-and-green bird, now living happy and free in the old oak.

"Todd and Natasha had noticed that a bird had somehow flown inside and gotten itself trapped in the ventilation pipes," Bethesda explained. "Janitor Steve noticed it, too, except he thought we had a ghost."

Principal Van Vreeland cocked an eyebrow at Janitor Steve, who shrugged, unembarrassed.

"Maybe we have birds *and* ghosts," he said.

The sad culprits took over their story again. Borrowing Janitor Steve's ladder from the basement and dragging it awkwardly down the hall *("I might have heard like a, like a scraping noise in the hall," Mr. Darlington had said)*, Todd unscrewed the duct cover, coaxed the swallow out, and carried it gently to the front door. But then, as he was folding up the ladder, disaster struck: Startled by a loud sound from down the hall—the *bang!* as Mr. Darlington kicked shut the front door of the school—Todd whipped around and the heavy foot of the ladder smashed the glass of the case. *A scrape, and then a bang, and then a crash.*

"Okay, well, that's, like, an amazing story, and I'm sure your bird friend is very happy," said Pamela, her hands on her hips. "But where's my trophy?"

"Well, uh—when the glass broke I sort of freaked out. Natasha knew about the bird, so I called her to help me clean up."

Natasha, in a low, weary voice, took over the story.

"I was at the mall when Todd called, getting my nails done before dinner." (Nobody asked what color, but if they had, Bethesda could have told them: red. Red as strawberry lollipops, red as blood.) "I biked over to the school, let myself in, and found Todd at the trophy case."

"Wait. Stop. Halt." Principal Van Vreeland held up one flat palm like a policewoman. "You let yourself in? But the door was now shut. Where did you get the key?"

Natasha grimaced. "Um . . . you see . . ."

Assistant Principal Jasper Ferrars, who since Principal Van Vreeland shook him off had been squatting in the aisle, sweating more and more profusely as the story went on, jumped to his feet. Shrieking incomprehensibly about a once-in-a-lifetime opportunity for a bass-baritone, he ran down the long aisle of the auditorium, up the steps of the stage, and out the door. Wordlessly, Principal Van Vreeland watched him go, then sighed, shook her head, and turned back to the children. "Go on."

The trophy case was full of glass, so Natasha carefully held the trophy while Todd pushed the shards out onto the floor. But when Natasha went to put the trophy back, they saw that she'd covered it with spots of still-sticky nail polish.

So now they had glass all over the floor, a broken case, and a gymnastics trophy that looked like it had the measles. The two friends, totally panicked, decided to bolt.

"I was already late for dinner," Natasha said. "So the plan was, I'd stick the trophy in my bag and take it to Pirate Sam's, then clean it later with nail polish remover."

"So you dragged the ladder back downstairs and got the heck out of there," Bethesda concluded. The crooks nodded miserably.

But of course they weren't crooks at all, Bethesda reflected, just two well-meaning eighth graders who had made a mistake. And then in trying to make things better they made them immeasurably worse.

"I knew it," Victor Glebe whispered glumly to Chester. "I knew she'd solve the mystery."

"But . . ." began Principal Van Vreeland, and then she and Pamela finished the sentence in unison: "Where's my trophy?"

Natasha blushed a deeper red than her nails had ever been. "Well, that's the thing. Somewhere between dinner at Pirate Sam's and my house, I, um . . . I lost it."

Pamela threw up her hands. The principal went pale, knees wobbling, and murmured, "Catch me, Jasper." Unfortunately, Jasper had fled the room, and the stunned principal landed with a dull thud on the thick auditorium carpet.

It was at that moment that Ivan Piccolini-Provokovsky strode purposefully into the room.

40

Pluck and Moxie; Gumption and Chutzpah

Mr. Ivan Piccolini-Provokovsky owed his rather extraordinary wealth to Ping-Pong paddles. Playing the game one afternoon with his niece, Lucy, he had noted with dismay that the paddle left something to be desired, in terms of grip strength; that same evening, in the workshop in his garage, he corrected the problem. If a new and improved Ping-Pong paddle doesn't sound like a way to become rather extraordinarily wealthy, consider that Ping-Pong happens to be the most popular sport in China—a nation of well over one billion people.

But long ago, long before he became extraordinarily wealthy, little Ivan Piccolini-Provokovsky was a middle school student prone to creative misbehavior. Like adding chocolate syrup to the cafeteria milk and reselling it at a margin. Or padlocking the teacher's lounge vending machine and ransoming the combination. Or gluing a construction-paper horn to the class hamster and selling pictures of The Amazing Unicorn Hamster to the local news. Now, reviewing his life from atop his giant Ping-Pong fortune, Mr. Piccolini-Provokovsky saw his middle school years with regret. Why had he only been punished? Why not encouraged to channel his imaginative impulses into more meaningful pursuits?

Now Ivan Piccolini-Provokovsky stood in the center aisle of the auditorium of Mary Todd Lincoln Middle School, one hand resting on the handle of a rolling suitcase, quasi-apologizing to Ida Finkleman for not returning her multiple emails. "I never let people know when I'm coming. Never! Element of surprise, get it?" He snapped his gum, tilted back his large, diamond-studded cowboy hat, and gave her a cheery thumbs-up. "Now! Where's this Chester character?"

Chester warily raised his hand.

"Step up here, fella. C'mon. Nothing to be afraid of. Yes, my boots are made of genuine one-hundred-percent alligator skin, but those gators have been dead a long time."

Principal Van Vreeland stirred from her faint,

struggled slowly to her feet, and whispered to Ms. Finkleman, "Is that who I think it is?" Ms. Finkleman nodded. "Yes. Yes, it is."

"All right," said Mr. Piccolini-Provokovsky, grabbing Chester's shoulders and looking him up and down. "It's my understanding that you've demonstrated certain qualities. Qualities like pluck and moxie. Gumption and chutzpah."

"Um . . ." said Chester. He shot a questioning glance at his best friend, Victor, who happened to have a really good vocabulary. Victor gave him a reassuring nod. "Um, thanks."

"Don't thank me. Thank this lady over here." He jerked his thumb at Ms. Finkleman, who beamed. Principal Van Vreeland whispered again. "Is he about to do what I think he's going to do?"

"Yes," said Ms. Finkleman, keeping her eyes on Chester and the fast-talking stranger in the alligator boots. "Yes, he is."

"It is an honor and a privilege and all that blah-di-dee-dah," Mr. Piccolini-Provokovsky continued rapidly, "to declare this school, the name of which I'll find out later, the winner of the Piccolini-Provokovsky Award for the Encouragement of Studential Excellence. And nobody better tell me that studential isn't a word, because I've heard it before."

Bethesda and Pamela, both of whom had raised their hands, lowered them again.

"The award, to be divided between school improvements and extracurricular activities, shall be in the sum of fifty thousand dollars."

He thrust a check at Chester Hu, whose eyes got as big and round as crash cymbals. The whole room burst into applause, with no one cheering louder than the "Save Taproot Valley" team (except Natasha and Todd, of course). "Woo!" shouted Suzie. "Bravo!" added Kevin. "That's what I'm talking about!" said Braxton. Marisol Pierce was too shy to shout, but she grinned from ear to ear and clapped till her hands were sore.

"Well, I gotta ramble," said Mr. Piccolini-Provokovsky suddenly, and pivoted on the heels of his lustrous boots. "Oh, shoot. One more thing. In addition to the money . . ." He bent over and unzipped the rolling suitcase.

"Is he going to say what I think he is?" said Principal Van Vreeland.

"Yes," Ms. Finkleman replied. "I think he is."

". . . the award includes this puppy right here."

The trophy was gleaming and massive, easily three

times as big as the one that had been lost. Principal Van Vreeland shrieked with girlish glee, like a child for whom Christmas has come at last.

All through Mr. Piccolini-Provokovsky's rapid-fire presentation, Bethesda kept her eyes on Natasha and Todd. She watched as they settled uneasily back into their seats, and imagined what they were feeling— that awful, gut-wrenching anticipation of big trouble to come, leavened by relief at having finally spilled the beans. That was one thing Bethesda had learned a time or two—as awful as it is to have to tell a painful truth, it sure beats carrying it around.

Bethesda Fielding, Master Detective, leaned back in her auditorium seat and let her tough-guy private-investigator face relax into a satisfied smile.

Case closed.

Epilogue

So the bus to Taproot Valley left that Monday morning after all, right on time and with just three empty seats.

The first empty seat was Natasha's, Principal Van Vreeland having decreed that, since she was the one who had lost the gymnastics trophy, she would be excluded from the trip.

The second empty seat was Todd Spolin's. "No way," he argued vigorously. "If she stays, I stay."

The third empty seat was the result of a special favor granted Chester Hu by Principal Van Vreeland, as a reward for bringing Mr. Piccolini-Provokovsky and his gigantic trophy to the school. Told that he could have anything he wanted, Chester had asked for a bazooka that shoots candy. When it was clarified that he could have anything he wanted, within reason, Chester had requested that his best friend, Victor, be allowed to skip out on the trip, no questions asked.

For the forty-five-minute bus ride to Taproot Valley, Tenny Boyer sat by himself way in the back, gazing absently out the window as the highway rolled by. Sliding into the seat beside him, Bethesda heard the tinny blare of something epic and punky from his earbuds; she guessed it was either Braid or Sunny Day Real Estate.

Bethesda leaned over and brazenly plucked the little white buds out of his ears.

"Hey!" Tenny protested.

"Sorry," she said, hurriedly replacing the snatched-away earbuds with her own. "But you gotta hear this."

Bethesda smiled with embarrassment as she hit play. She had recorded the whole thing on the computer, which she didn't really know how to do properly. But what the song lacked in quality, it more than made up for in spirit. "Because I was wrong, so very wrong," she sang, accompanied by energetic strumming on her dad's old guitar. "I wrote you this terrible song!"

It was an off-key, off-kilter performance, full of purposefully awful singing and purposefully awful lyrics, like where she rhymed "I stuck my nose in" with "so forgive me, is what I'm proposin'." After a minute or two, Tenny's mask of annoyance dissolved and he cracked up, stabbing for the pause button. "Please!" he yelped. "Make it stop!"

"So you forgive me?"

He nodded, laughing helplessly. "Make it stop! Make it stop!"

Tenny told Bethesda the whole story that evening, during the half hour of free time the eighth graders were afforded after their daylong "ecological hike" and before that night's recreational activity. (Which was, as it turned out, a giddy, exhilarating, and exhausting game of capture the flag, organized by Coach Vasouvian, that they'd still be talking about years later. It would emerge as one of the famous facts about the Taproot Valley trip, along with Dr. Capshaw's nonstop reciting of Robert Frost poems during the apple-cider demonstration, and Braxton Lashey stomping around after lights-out in his bear costume.)

Tenny had *not* been expelled from St. Francis Xavier. He hadn't set any fires, or driven any cars into any lakes. After just a couple weeks, right when he was getting the hang of the place, his parents had pulled him out because they were getting divorced.

"I guess it's not, like, one of those really easy,

everybody's-all-cool-with-everybody divorces," Tenny said. They were sitting together on two of the oversized deck chairs that lined the edge of Lake Taproot. As he talked, Tenny kept his eyes locked on the lake, where minnows dived and darted in little clusters. "So there's a big fight about money, and I guess St. Francis costs a ton."

"Tenny . . ."

"Yeah. So, anyway. I really didn't want anyone to know. Didn't really feel like talking about it, you know? I did call Ms. Finkleman, though, when—when it was all getting going."

Bethesda nodded. Of course.

"The real bummer is, I was sort of digging the place, a little." Bethesda thought about the ways Tenny was different since he came back: polite Tenny, logical Tenny . . . but still good ol' Tenny, just the same.

They stood up from the deck chairs and flipped a couple flat rocks into the lake, rippling the murky surface and startling the minnows. The solution to the great mystery of Tenny's return to Mary Todd Lincoln Middle School had at last been revealed, but Bethesda felt a lot less satisfaction than she had anticipated.

"Let's go, people!" boomed Coach Vasouvian's big voice, and they ran off to play.

✦ ✦ ✦

That left just one more mystery, the one that had caused Bethesda so much trouble. Who had scrawled the letters IOM on the lower left-hand wall of the Achievement Alcove . . . and why?

She never would have found out if they hadn't crossed paths with the eighth graders from Grover Cleveland, whose week at Taproot Valley was beginning just as the Mary Todd Lincoln week was ending. Everyone was milling around the parking lot outside the Welcome Center, sizing each other up as kids from different schools always do, when a Grover Cleveland girl named Sue Park ran up to Marisol.

"Oh my god! You're one of the girls from the Save Taproot Valley video!"

She pleaded for an autograph, but Marisol pointed her over to Chester. "That's the guy you want."

Sue Park was a bit disappointed, even more so when Chester had autographed the piece of loose-leaf she shoved in his face.

"What does this say? Chapter? Your name is Chapter Hut?"

As the Grover Cleveland kids were rounded up and marched inside, and the Mary Todd Lincoln kids piled back on their bus, Bethesda looked from Chester to Marisol, and back to Chester. *Of course!* It wasn't IOM scrawled on the back wall of the Achievement Alcove, directly below Marisol's charcoal drawing of a fruit bowl. It was an I, and then a heart—a badly drawn, terrible-handwriting heart—and then an M. It had nothing to do with the trophy. Before it was stolen, probably before Pamela even won the thing, Chester had snuck into the Achievement Alcove and left a secret tribute to his all-time favorite artist: *I heart Marisol.*

During the long bus ride home, Bethesda listened as Marisol and Chester laughingly recounted the game of capture the flag; she watched Tenny sitting in the very back row, fingerpicking his acoustic guitar; she saw Reenie, with no book in her lap, chatting with Bessie about the animal they'd chased up Taproot Hill. They'd decided it was either a gila monster or the world's last surviving dragon.

Bethesda never told Chester what she'd deduced. She never revealed the solution to Tenny, or Reenie, or anyone.

Some mysteries, she decided, are supposed to stay mysteries.

Acknowledgments

If you're like me, and you always read the dedication page and wonder, *Who's that person?*, please know that Raedina Winters was my father's mother. She died in the summer of 2010 at age ninety-eight, a couple weeks after giving her final tap-dance lesson. She was brilliant, funny, and beautiful, and she loved her family.

Thanks to everyone who read and enjoyed *The Secret Life of Ms. Finkleman*, and all the kids I got to hang out with promoting the book—particularly the boisterous ragamuffins at the Anderson School, P. S. 334.

Thanks to the many friends who may have caught glimpses of their names, personalities, or favorite bands in this book or the last one. Any similarity between Chester Hu and Dan Chu is strictly coincidental, except that I love them both a lot.

A thousand million thanks to my agent, Molly Lyons at Joelle Delbourgo Associates, and to everyone at HarperCollins who worked so hard to make my work look good and find its way into the bookstores; especially my editor, Sarah Sevier, who more than anyone helped me create the world of Mary Todd Lincoln Middle School.

Last and probably most, a million trillion thanks to my darling family: Diana, Rosalie, and Isaac Winters.